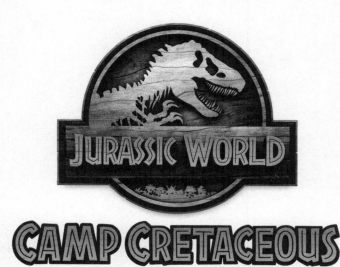

CAMP CRETACEOUS

rhcbooks.com

ISBN 978-0-593-31027-4 (hardcover) — ISBN 978-0-593-31028-1 (ebook)

Printed in the United States of America   10 9 8 7 6 5 4 3 2 1

Random House Children's Books supports the First Amendment and
celebrates the right to read.

Volume Three:
The Junior Novelization

Adapted by Steve Behling
Cover illustrated by Patrick Spaziante

CHAPTER ONE

"**G**oodbye, Jurassic World!"

Darius tilted his head to see the tattered Jurassic World banner fluttering in the wind. Ben stood next to him, at the base of the mast. They were no longer on Isla Nublar, no longer at Camp Cretaceous.

The makeshift raft rose and fell with the ocean waves as Darius and his fellow campers set sail from Jurassic World.

"Goodbye, Bumpy," Ben said, staring back at the shore. Bumpy the Ankylosaurus, Ben's friend, stood there, whimpering and wailing. The sounds of the distraught creature filled Ben's ears.

Darius put a reassuring hand on Ben's shoulder. He was just about to say something when Kenji shouted, "Woooo! Ha-hah! See ya *never*, stupid dino island!"

Kenji did a victory dance next to Darius, like he

had just scored the winning touchdown at his fifth Super Bowl.

While the others joked around, Brooklynn stared off into the horizon. "Um, guys?" she said.

Everyone turned to see what Brooklynn was looking at—an enormous wave about to bear down on them.

"It's okay!" Darius said. "The wind's strong, so we can just power through!" He reached for the sail, but the moment he touched it, the wind turned the sail around and started to tear it away from the mast.

The kids immediately grabbed for the sail, but the wind was too strong. The sail was ripped from their hands as the shadow of the giant wave fell over them.

"Brace yourselves!" Darius commanded as everyone screamed.

While the island full of hungry dinosaurs had yet to stop the kids of Camp Cretaceous, the ocean wave certainly had stopped them. The campers were helpless before its might. The wave had washed their raft all the way back to the shore of Isla Nublar.

With no other choice, they picked themselves

up and trudged all the way back to Camp Cretaceous. Of course, things had changed a little since the last time they were there. Before the kids tried to escape the island on the raft, they had raided the luxury campsite of Tiff and Mitch, the so-called ecotourists who turned out to be dinosaur trophy hunters. They got a cool recliner and took the food that remained. They'd also built up their camp more, adding a second floor to their tree-house home.

"Bumpy, we're back!" Ben shouted as they re-entered camp. The heavily built dinosaur exploded from the foliage, knocking Ben to the ground.

"Missed you, too!" Ben said.

"Circle up, guys! Camp meeting!" Darius called, and everyone gathered around as he drew on a chalkboard. "On the plus side, still no sign of Compys around camp," he said.

The Compsognathuses had been a constant danger the whole time the kids had been on the island. The dinosaurs were small, and while one or two weren't really a problem, a whole bunch of hungry Compys were.

"On the minus side," Darius continued, "raft-escape attempt number one was, um . . ."

"Didn't work," Brooklynn said. "We're out of options. Think. What *haven't* we tried yet?"

"I still think a raft or boat is the way to go," Darius said, trying to keep the group focused. "All we need is a better sail—"

"Sails, rafts, boats," Kenji snorted. "It's a shame we can't just go up to Lookout Point and hang glide all the way to Costa Rica."

Darius looked at Kenji, his eyes getting big. "Wait. What's Lookout Point?"

"It's up in the mountains to the west," Kenji explained. "They've got hang gliders and everything. I used to go there all the time."

"Hang gliders," Darius said. "As in, pieces of material that are *literally* designed to catch the wind?"

"Yeah, so?" Kenji replied, not making the mental leap, as usual.

Darius and Brooklynn broke into huge grins. Sammy and Yasmina high-fived each other.

At last, Kenji nodded slowly as though he got it, too.

"Welcome to Lookout Point!" Kenji exclaimed, gesturing grandly at the steep mountain in front of them. "Well, to be fair, Lookout Point is up *there.*"

"So how do we get up there?" Darius asked.

Kenji motioned toward a gondola that could carry passengers from the base of the mountain all the way to the summit. "The Sky Gondola, usually," he said. "But with the power out, you'll have to go on foot. Shouldn't be too bad, probs just a one-to-five-day trek. I'll hold down the fort here while you guys hike—"

Before Kenji could finish, the gondola clicked and buzzed. Then it began to move!

"Ta-da!" Brooklynn said as she stood at a control panel on the side of the gondola's loading platform.

"Welcome to the Lookout Point Gondola, solar powered by Masrani Global's green energy program," a recording of a Park announcer said over the gondola's speakers.

Sammy and Kenji took one car, and Brooklynn and Yasmina squeezed into another.

"Guess it's you and me, Ben," Darius said.

But Ben shook his head and pointed to Bumpy. "Bumpy can't fit in there."

"Oh," Darius said. "Well, we can just leave her behind—"

"No," Ben said forcefully.

"Is there something . . . wrong?" Darius asked.

"Nope, go ahead. I'm fine," Ben said, sounding anything but.

Darius knew that something was up. So he

grabbed a walkie-talkie. "Kenji?" he said into the receiver. "You guys go ahead and get the hang glider. I'll stay down here with Ben."

The gondolas finally arrived at the top of Lookout Point. The area was flat, and large boulders dotted the landscape. Across from the gondola lift was a scenic viewpoint with a guardrail overlooking the island below. Opposite that were several large hang gliders chained to the ground.

Sammy and Kenji jumped right out of their car and ran to the overlook. Then Brooklynn and Yasmina disembarked.

"Ya know, once you get past the 'imminent death lurking around every corner' thing, this place really is paradise," Sammy said.

"I'm just saying that if there is something bothering you, we can fix it," Darius said.

"You're gonna 'fix' my feelings?" Ben said, frustrated.

"I knew it!" Darius said, oblivious to his friend's anger. "Something *is* bothering you! You can tell me! What? What is it? Are you—"

"I don't want to leave Bumpy again!" Ben shouted. "When I got back to camp and I saw her, I realized it was a mistake to leave her. She's always been there for me, and then . . . I just abandoned her. I can't do it again. I just *can't*."

Darius was quiet, not knowing exactly what to say. He watched as Bumpy approached and nudged Ben with her head. The nudge nearly knocked Ben to the ground as he turned to face the dinosaur, hugging her tight.

"Ben, she'll be okay without you," Darius said, struggling to find the words.

"Of course she will. It's just that . . . ," Ben said, his voice trailing off. "I don't know if *I'll* be okay. I appreciate what you're trying to do, Darius, but some things . . . some things just can't be fixed."

"Relax," Brooklynn said, looking at the lock that held the chain—and the hang gliders—to the ground. "I can totally pick that lock."

"That'll take forever," Yasmina said. "All *I* need is a rock." She walked away from Brooklynn, searching for a suitable stone to use.

"Almost . . . ," Brooklynn said, working the lock.

"Where's a good one?" Yasmina said to herself, still looking for a good lock-smashing rock. She found one that might work, but something about it wasn't . . . right. Suddenly, she froze in place.

"Kenji, look at this, quick!" Sammy said. She was using a pair of mounted binoculars at the scenic overlook. Grabbing Kenji, Sammy shoved him right in front of one of the viewers so they could both see.

"What am I looking at?" Kenji asked.

"Keep going, keep going. . . . It was right over . . . there! See?"

Kenji saw what Sammy was talking about, but he couldn't believe it. They were staring at a secluded inlet and something beached against nearby rocks in the ocean.

A yacht.

"Tiff and Mitch's boat!" Kenji and Sammy said in unison.

Brooklynn worked the lock, and it opened with a satisfying pop!

"Ha!" Brooklynn laughed. "So much for taking forever."

Brooklynn turned around hoping to enjoy her little victory, but Yasmina wasn't paying attention.

"Yaz, what's wrong?" Brooklynn asked.

Yasmina turned and showed the rock to Brook-lynn.

"These aren't rocks," Yasmina said. Brooklynn's eyes grew wide. "They're eggs."

Then a loud HISS filled the air as a razor-toothed Dimorphodon flew over the edge of the overlook, landing right in front of Sammy and Kenji!

Backing away slowly, Kenji said, "Nice creepy bird thing . . ."

The Dimorphodon shrieked in response, baring its teeth. Sammy and Kenji backed away, but the Dimorphodon followed, walking along the rocks with its talons. The kids tried to take another step but felt something blocking their way. They were now backed up against the guardrail!

The Dimorphodon let out another earsplitting shriek, followed by another, like it was sounding an alarm. . . .

"Back to the gondolas!" Yasmina screamed as a flock of Dimorphodons headed their way.

CHAPTER TWO

At last, a gondola arrived, and Kenji and Sammy jumped inside and slammed the lock button.

WHAM!

A Dimorphodon hit the glass, denied its prey.

The two jumped back, startled.

The flock of Dimorphodons were almost directly above Lookout Point and had started to circle. Beneath them, Brooklynn and Yasmina were dragging a big, ungainly hang glider toward the gondola platform.

"They're closing in!" Brooklynn shouted, watching helplessly as the Dimorphodon flock shrieked and descended upon them. The pterosaurs landed on the ground, placing themselves right between the girls and the gondola lift.

"Is there another way down?" Yasmina asked.

A huge Dimorphodon crawled out from the flock, hissing loudly, moving closer.

Brooklynn and Yasmina looked at the each other, and then their eyes drifted to the hang glider. They looked at each other once again.

"No other choice," Brooklynn said.

"Nope," Yasmina agreed.

Instinctively, the girls grasped either side of the hang-glider bar, snapping each other onto the safety rope. Then they ran toward the edge of Lookout Point, screaming.

Their feet pounded on the rocky surface, moving faster and faster until at last the girls had run out of ground. They had gone over the edge as the hang glider caught a breeze and kept them aloft.

"We're flying," Brooklynn stated. "We're so cool!"

"Right?!" Yasmina agreed as the girls grinned and laughed.

The hang glider sailed along as they flew above a clearing in the jungle below. They could see Darius and Ben!

Just when it seemed like everything was going to be fine, the girls heard a loud shriek behind them. The Dimorphodons were coming. One broke from the flock and headed right for them. Brooklynn bit her lip, then said, "Lean left on three! One . . . two . . . three!!"

They leaned to the left, and the hang glider tilted just enough for the dive-bombing Dimorphodon to miss them!

"Incoming!" Yasmina called out as another Dimorphodon approached. "To the right—now!"

The girls leaned right, evading the Dimorphodon.

The Dimorphodon flock continued to shriek as Yasmina looked ahead. "Head for that cloud!" she said as Brooklynn steered the hang glider toward the puffy mass. Once they were inside of the cloud, the sound of the Dimorphodons seemed to fade.

"I think we lost 'em!" Brooklynn said as Yasmina whooped. The girls high-fived each other with their free hands, and when they emerged from the cloud, they could no longer see the Dimorphodons.

Now all they had to do was find a way to land, which they probably could have done if there wasn't a sudden ripping noise as a Dimorphodon swooped in and tore a hole in the hang glider. The creature snapped at them as the hang glider tumbled toward the jungle.

The Dimorphodon ceased its attack before the hang glider crashed into the trees. Darius, Ben, and Bumpy sprinted through the underbrush, trying to get to their friends as quickly as possible. When they emerged in a clearing, Darius ran ahead.

Almost immediately, Ben sensed that something was wrong. Instinctively, he looked toward the sky, and then he saw it.

"Darius! Watch out!" Ben yelled as a Dimorphodon swooped down from above. It let out a wild, hair-raising SHRIEK as it headed right for Darius!

Ben didn't even think. His body went right into action mode, and he hurled himself at Darius, knocking his friend out of the way of the rapidly approaching reptile. Both kids hit the ground hard, just as the Dimorphodon buzzed overhead. They could feel the wind from its wings. And they were relieved that the creature's terrible talons had narrowly missed them.

But that didn't mean the Dimorphodon was done with them yet. The flying reptile came back around, picking up speed. It was going to dive again! Before Ben or Darius could react, the Dimorphodon closed the space between them. Talons flashed out, and Darius flinched.

Suddenly, Bumpy whipped her mighty tail, striking the Dimorphodon just as it was about to strike! The flying reptile let out another shriek, this time one of pain, as it crashed to the ground. Darius got to his feet and stood next to Ben, who was holding a large stick, ready to fight.

Bumpy narrowed her eyes, glaring at the Dimorphodon. It was now three against one!

The Dimorphodon took a moment. It cocked its head from side to side as if assessing the situation. Then it slowly backed away from the boys and Bumpy. The creature flapped its wings and, with a loud, unearthly HISS, flew off into the sky.

For a moment, neither Darius nor Ben said a word, but both of them exhaled sighs of relief. They couldn't believe their luck, although it wasn't entirely luck. The kids had learned so much about survival since they had been stranded at Camp Cretaceous. What to do, what not to do. There was some skill involved in this, too.

As Darius felt his stomach unclench, he heard the sound of a slow clap.

"Wowwwwwwww!"

It was Brooklynn! She and Yasmina had climbed down from the tree they had crashed into.

"That was *very* impressive," Yasmina said.

"I mean, not as impressive as me and Yaz literally *flying* away from danger," Brooklynn added.

The girls looked at each other, grinning from ear to ear. Then they fist-bumped.

Darius looked at Ben as if to say, "Um, okay, so is this a thing that they're doing now? And since when?"

While the girls basked in their moment of triumph, Kenji and Sammy rushed to join them. They had made it safely to the base of the mountain in their gondola. Sammy hugged everyone, and Kenji did a victory dance.

"I love it when we're alive!" Sammy said, brimming with joy.

"Yeahhh!" Kenji shouted. "Take *that,* dino island! Whoo!"

Yasmina took a deep breath, grateful to be alive. She looked at Brooklynn and nodded. "It was a team effort," she said, and she meant it.

Brooklynn returned the smile, silently acknowledging the compliment. The two might have had their issues before, but the hang-gliding incident had brought them closer together. (Surviving an aerial Dimorphodon attack had that effect on people.)

Darius checked out the hang glider that was stuck in the tree, focusing on the ripped material. "It's a little torn, but we can fix it," he said. "And it's gonna be a perfect sail for our next boat!"

Kenji and Sammy immediately exchanged looks and, with tremendous excitement, shouted, "BOAT!"

Darius, Ben, Brooklynn, and Yasmina looked at their friends as if to say, "I have no idea what you're talking about."

CHAPTER THREE

The sun was setting, and Darius thought that the jungle looked simply amazing. The group was heading back to Camp Cretaceous, but this time, they were full of high spirits and hope.

"Man, remember when we ran straight at that freaky flying dinosaur?" Kenji said.

"Nope," Sammy replied, not bothering to say that it was really a flying reptile. "Already blocked it out!"

Kenji grinned. "That's why I'm here to remind you."

Sammy covered her ears and started to laugh. "Nooooo!" she cried.

As Kenji tormented Sammy with memories of Dimorphodons and gondolas, Brooklynn took the opportunity to get to know Yasmina better.

"So tell me about track meetings," Brooklynn said. "What are they like?"

"Meetings?" Yasmina asked, laughing. "What, you think I run laps in a conference room?"

"C'monnnnn," Brooklynn replied. "Can I get a few points for trying?"

Yasmina couldn't help but smile at her friend's mistake. Then she proceeded to tell Brooklynn about track meets, and Brooklynn peppered her with question after question.

Meanwhile, Darius walked with Ben and Bumpy, his mind racing. "And best of all, Tiff and Mitch's boat is plenty big enough for Bumpy to get on board!" He explained that the boat would have no trouble taking them off Isla Nublar.

Ben nodded but didn't say anything.

"Told ya," Darius said, nudging Ben. "There's always a fix."

"I'll never doubt you again," Ben replied. For a moment, his expression seemed distant. Then at last, Ben's face broke into a smile. Darius was happy. It meant a lot to see Ben in good spirits.

Darius looked away as he went back to planning the departure from Camp Cretaceous in his head. That's when the smile faded from Ben's face. Unlike Darius, he wasn't so sure that everything was going to work out.

As the group continued through the jungle, they remained blissfully unaware of the shadow that emerged from the thick foliage.

The Ceratosaurus watched them through the foliage, silently. It had been following them for hours. And now it was ready to strike. The muscles in its powerful legs coiled, but before it could launch its attack, something grabbed it.

Something . . . bigger than it was. Bigger and deathly silent.

It dragged the Ceratosaurus into the shadows.

"It's so close," Yasmina said. The group had gone back to Camp Cretaceous, gathered the supplies they needed, and then made the trek down to Mitch and Tiff's yacht.

"Have you ever seen anything so beautiful?" Kenji wondered.

"It is really there?" Brooklynn asked. "I mean . . . we're not just *imagining* it, right?"

"Nope," Darius said, trying to sound reassuring. "It's really there."

Sammy turned to look at her friends and was glad to see Bumpy with them. "Well, what are we waiting for?" she said as she picked up a Jurassic World tote bag. "I brought our swimsuits from camp. No need to get our clothes all wet getting out there."

Then she dug into the bag and started to hand out swimsuits to everyone.

"Stay sharp," Darius said, keeping a watchful eye. "For all we know, Tiff or the Baryonyxes could still be around."

Yasmina nodded. "Hard to tell which is scarier."

The kids looked at each other and nodded in agreement. Darius's warning injected a dose of reality into the situation. Sammy returned to handing out the swimsuits, but she did so now while looking all around her for any sign of danger.

Once the kids had put on their swim gear, they headed down to the water. Darius took a deep breath and said a silent goodbye to the island. Then he put a foot in the water, followed by another. The others did the same, and soon they were all swimming out to Mitch and Tiff's yacht.

Darius was kind of surprised that there wasn't anything lurking in the water, waiting to get them. Based on everything they had experienced on the island, he half expected something to come rising out of the sea and swallow them whole!

Thankfully, that didn't happen.

Soon, they found themselves next to the yacht. The kids took turns climbing onto the boat and settled in.

"No sign of anything or anyone," Ben said cautiously.

Brooklynn looked around the yacht, and her eyes drifted downward. She saw huge claw marks on the deck beneath her feet, and she gulped.

"And yet, still super creepy," she said.

Sammy was the first one to make it to the bridge, where she found signs of an obvious struggle. There were claw marks, cracked windows, and broken instruments on the control panel. She sighed, getting nothing—not even static—out of the busted radio.

"The control panel's busted up. Looks like there's no navigation," Darius said. Then he checked the fuel gauge and saw that the red needle hovered just above EMPTY. "And it's almost out of gas."

"Are you sure?" Sammy asked. "Did you tap it? They *always* tap it."

Sammy moved over to the fuel gauge and gently tapped the glass with her finger. The red needle that was *so close* to being on EMPTY jumped.

Now it was ENTIRELY on EMPTY.

"Well . . . now we're *really* sure," Sammy said, disappointed.

"So we've got a boat," Ben said. "We just can't *use* the boat."

Darius thought for a second, then pointed out the cracked window. "The northwest dock is just around that bend. If we can make it there, maybe we can find gas and whatever else we need to get us off the island."

CHAPTER FOUR

Darius climbed down from the controls to the main deck. There, he saw Brooklynn. He was about to say something when a strange rustling sound came from below deck.

Darius and Brooklynn froze in their tracks. Had Tiff survived? Was she coming out from below deck right now, ready to take back her yacht? Or was it a Baryonyx? Though that was less likely given their size. But like Yasmina said, it was hard to tell which would be worse.

Brooklynn held her breath—ready for anything—when the door suddenly burst open!

"Boo!"

Both Darius and Brooklynn shrieked and stumbled backward, ready to run. Their stunned looks gave way to annoyance as they saw Kenji emerge from the doorway.

"Gotcha!" Kenji said, laughing.

"Kenji!" Brooklynn said.

"Not funny, dude!" Darius added. "You scared the—"

"I know," Kenji cackled. "It was *awesome*! You should've seen your faces! Price . . . less!"

"The height of comedy," Ben said. "I'm gonna head back to shore. Bumpy and I will meet you guys at the dock."

"Guess the only question is, who's driving the boat?" Yasmina asked.

Kenji smiled. "You mean, whose dad has a yacht club membership and just found this killer hat?"

Then he placed something on his head . . . a captain's hat.

"Captain Kenji, at your service!" he said, saluting.

And while Kenji seemed to relish the idea of being a captain, nobody else was sure it was such a great idea.

A while later, Darius found himself standing on the dock, along with Brooklynn, Sammy, Yasmina, and Kenji. The yacht was now fully docked.

"Not a bad parking job, if I do say so myself," Kenji said. "And I will."

"You don't *park* a boat," Yasmina said, rolling

her eyes. "You *dock* it."

Kenji looked at Yasmina, then pointed at his hat. "Sure you wanna sass the captain?" he asked. Then, in a sing-song voice, he said, "It's a long swim home!"

Yasmina just smirked in reply.

Ben approached the group, with Bumpy at his side.

"Hey, friends," Sammy said. "How was your walk?"

"Great," Ben said, and it sounded like he meant it. "Zero dinos. And even better, the dock's surrounded by a fence. I locked it up after Bumpy and I came through."

"So we're safe," Brooklynn said. "That's new."

Darius nodded. "It's getting late," he said. "We might as well rest up here. We can scavenge for gas and supplies in the morning."

As he sat on a deck chair next to Brooklynn, Darius thought that maybe they could, just this once, relax. Maybe they really were safe.

"We're not just leaving the island tomorrow," Brooklynn said as she gestured to the yacht. "We're leaving in style."

"Gotta admit, I'm lovin' this yacht life," Darius

agreed. "But there is still one thing we need to do before we go. Prank Kenji back for scaring us."

"Ooh, you know I'm down for that," Brooklynn said, her eyes narrowing.

Without looking, the two fist-bumped. "Got it! We steal his captain's hat," Darius said.

"Uh-huh! And then?!" Brooklynn asked, looking forward to whatever mischief her friend had in mind.

In that moment, Darius realized that he didn't have an "and then."

"We . . . don't give it back?" he suggested, hoping this sounded like a better idea than it was.

Brooklynn's face fell, and Darius said, "Yeah, lame. Sorry. When you've got an older brother like Brand, you're usually the prank victim, not the prank planner."

Brooklynn thought for a moment. "It's gotta be something epic, or he'll never leave us alone. What if we slowly and methodically make Kenji believe he never existed? Then, just when he's on the verge of total madness, we'll be like, 'Gotcha!'"

Darius stared at Brooklynn. "Might be too intense? Maybe we—"

Before he could suggest something a little less disturbing, there came a rapid POP POP POP sound, startling Darius and Brooklynn.

Kenji emerged from behind, throwing party poppers that he had found on Mitch and Tiff's yacht.

"Seriously, Kenji?" Darius said.

"I know, right? Too easy!" Kenji replied.

"All ideas are back on the table," Darius said as Kenji walked away. "The more intense, the better."

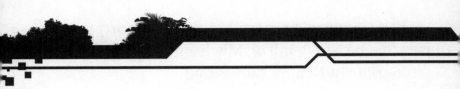

CHAPTER FIVE

***K**A-THUNK!*

They felt the boat shudder. Darius nearly lost his balance.

"What was that?" he wondered.

Ben nodded at a slack rope hanging over the side of the boat, wrapped around a cleat on the pier to keep the yacht from drifting off. "Maybe the *captain* forgot to tie the boat down tight."

"That's a thing?" Kenji asked.

"So we probably just drifted and bumped against the pier," Sammy said.

"It's more than just a bump," Darius said as he pointed to a large gash on the yacht's hull, right above the water line. "This won't wait till tomorrow. We gotta patch this tonight, before—"

"The boat sinks," Kenji said.

Brooklynn turned away from the yacht, looking

at the warehouses, cargo containers, and crates that were all around them. "There's gotta be some tools or boating supplies around here we can scavenge."

Darius nodded as he glanced up at the sky. "Let's hurry. It's getting dark, and the fog's rolling in. We should split up so we can cover more ground quickly."

Yasmina didn't have to be told twice, and she took off like a shot. Bumpy followed her as the others set off in search of supplies as well.

The fog was getting thicker as the sun went down.

The fog had grown so dense that Yasmina was beginning to have trouble seeing. She was glad to have Bumpy by her side. The two had come across a large shipping container. Yasmina approached it cautiously and yanked on the doors, but they wouldn't budge. Then she walked over to the next container and did the same thing. Still no luck. Bumpy grumbled.

"Just chill, Bumpy," Yasmina said. "This could take a while."

Yasmina turned around to give Bumpy a reassuring pet on the head but was surprised to see that the Ankylosaurus had already wandered off.

"Oof!"

Darius was trying to navigate his way along the dock and through the fog when he bumped into a perimeter fence. Then he spotted something dark and small on the ground. Darius walked over and saw that it was a toolbox. Opening it, he found a roll of duct tape.

It was better than nothing, so Darius put the tape in his pocket. As he stood up, he noticed something that made his blood run cold: a gaping hole in the fence.

They weren't alone.

Sammy was walking along the dock when she heard a grunt and saw a tail swinging in the fog. She smiled and called out, "Bumpy, is that you? Are you lost in the fog, girl?"

There was no response. Sammy didn't really expect one anyway.

"Sit tight. I'm coming your way!" Sammy said as she took off toward the sound of the dinosaur.

Brooklynn had made her way to a warehouse by the dock. She took out the master key card she had removed from Dr. Wu's lab weeks ago and held it up to the warehouse doors. The only problem was, there was no scanner. The doors were padlocked.

Shrugging her shoulders, Brooklynn put the key card away and then pulled a bobby pin from her hair. She had started to pick the lock when something suddenly grabbed her from behind.

Brooklynn gasped—but it was only Darius.

"Something broke in through the fence," Darius whispered. "We all need to get to the boat, now!"

Brooklynn's eyes went wide as he pulled her warily into the fog.

Squinting, Darius saw something moving ahead. "There's Ben!" he said, nudging Brooklynn.

"Ben!" Brooklynn called. "Over here!"

Then something stirred, and Darius saw a pair of Ouranosauruses emerge. The enormous creatures didn't seem to be paying them any attention.

"It's okay," Darius said. "They're just Ouranosauruses."

"By 'just,' I'm guessing you mean herbivores?" Brooklynn asked.

"They're big," Darius replied, "but they're pretty much harmless—"

Suddenly, the Ouranosauruses became agitated and started to swing their thick tails.

"Do *they* know that?" Ben called out as the dinosaurs charged the three of them!

Yasmina tugged on the doors of another container. Unsurprisingly, it was locked. She was just about to move on when she saw a crowbar sitting on top of a crate. She walked over to the crowbar just as an Ouranosaurus appeared.

Yasmina grabbed the crowbar. Pressing herself against the doors of the container, she inched toward the distant corner and looked around. Her heart sank when she saw *another* Ouranosaurus coming her way.

She was trapped. She grasped the crowbar, ready to fight. Her eyes drifted upward as she waited for the Ouranosauruses to approach, and then a thought occurred to her. Using the crowbar like a grappling hook, Yasmina caught the top of the container with the clawed edge. She pulled herself up, narrowly avoiding the two Ouranosauruses.

One of the dinosaurs slowly looked up and saw Yasmina. It started to whip the container with its tail, and the other Ouranosaurus joined in.

Thinking fast, Yasmina took a running leap, crossing the gap between containers. Then she kept on running and jumping.

Kenji had been wandering the dock and had turned up nothing so far. Then he heard a low growl that seemed to echo in the fog that surrounded him. He stopped walking through the shipping containers, completely freaked out.

Then a crate slid right past him as if it was possessed by ghosts!

"Who's out there?" Kenji demanded.

He heard the growl once more as an angry Ouranosaurus peeked through the fog, menacing Kenji. He fell to the ground and stared up at the dinosaur. The creature stared back, growling, until they were almost nose to nose! Kenji barely managed to scoot away as the dinosaur came in for the kill.

A second later, Kenji was back on his feet, running through the fog with the Ouranosaurus in pursuit. Just when it seemed like the dinosaur was going to catch Kenji, there was a loud CLANG on the ground behind the Ouranosaurus, like something falling. The dinosaur turned its head, walking back to investigate.

Kenji looked up and saw Yasmina standing atop a container.

"Help me down!" she whispered.

"Are you crazy?" Kenji said. "Help me *up*!"

He turned his head to see the Ouranosaurus coming back.

Yasmina pointed at a crate. Kenji shoved it against the container. She jumped onto it, then hit the ground. Before the Ouranosaurus could make it back, the two were already off and running—right into Darius and the others!

"Kenji! You're okay!" Brooklynn said.

"Wait, where's Sammy?" Yasmina asked.

"And Bumpy?" Ben added.

Sammy found Bumpy in the fog. The dinosaur snorted as Sammy approached. She was agitated. Slowly it dawned on Sammy that Bumpy wasn't upset with her, but at something else. She turned her head and saw the problem—an Ouranosaurus was creeping up on them!

Bumpy stepped in front of Sammy and began to bellow. She was protecting Sammy!

The Ouranosaurus and Bumpy charged each other!

"Bumpy!" Sammy screamed as she watched the two dinosaurs. Before they could collide, Bumpy twisted her body, skidding sideways toward the Ouranosaurus. The Ankylosaurus slammed right into the other dinosaur's lower legs. The taller dinosaur lost her footing and fell over!

Immediately, Sammy ran past the dinosaur as it thrashed on the ground. She and Bumpy took off into the fog. They kept on running, and Sammy was surprised to hear another sound that wasn't a growl—it sounded like someone calling her name!

"Bumpy! Sammy!"

It was Ben!

A moment later, Sammy saw Ben come out of the fog with Darius, Brooklynn, Kenji, and Yasmina.

"You guys okay?" Yasmina asked, worried.

"Yeah," Sammy said. "But there's—"

"Mad dinos. We know," Darius said. "We gotta get on the boat and cast off!"

The Ouranosauruses followed the kids, but the campers had already made it down the pier.

Everyone had boarded the ship except Darius and Brooklynn. They watched as Bumpy clambered onto the yacht, and Darius noticed something truly disturbing. With Bumpy's added weight, the hole in the yacht's hull was now dipping perilously close to the water line.

"We've gotta patch this thing!" Darius said.

Then he turned to Brooklynn and pulled out the duct tape that he had found earlier. "Can you do anything with this tape?"

Brooklynn tore some tape from the roll and said, "Only everything."

The Ouranosauruses were heading down the pier now, coming closer to the yacht.

"Grab whatever you can to plug it up," Brooklynn said. "This won't hold long, but it's all we got!"

The kids moved with purpose as Yasmina threw towels and swimsuits down to Darius. He plugged them into the hole, but it wasn't enough.

Kenji looked around to see what else he could throw, but there was nothing.

Darius stretched duct tape over the hole and hoped for the best. "Get us out of here!" he yelled.

Kenji wasted no time in racing to the bridge, moving behind the ship's wheel. On the pier below, Brooklynn was sealing the hole with the tape.

"They're coming!" Sammy said nervously, and Brooklynn knew that the Ouranosauruses were closer than ever.

"Let's go!" Brooklynn shouted as she placed the last piece of tape. "Kenji, drive!"

The Ouranosauruses reached the end of the pier just as Darius and Brooklynn jumped aboard the yacht that was already pulling away. The dinosaurs stopped and bellowed!

"I cut the engine to save whatever fuel's left," Kenji said as the dock faded away into the fog. "We are officially adrift," Kenji said.

"It still doesn't make sense," Darius pondered. "First, the Compys disappear from camp, then peaceful herbivores attack us and take over the dock—an area they shouldn't even care about."

"Things are definitely getting next-level weird," Brooklynn observed.

"Yeah," Kenji said. "Dinos *never* go bonkers at Jurassic World."

Brooklynn grinned as Darius said, "It's more than that. It's like the whole island is . . . out of balance somehow. But why?"

The jungle was quiet. There was a frightening stillness—not a Compsognathus to be heard moving through the brush, nor the shriek of a Dimorphodon soaring overhead.

The Park's original Ouranosaurus habitat had been occupied not too long ago. But now all that remained were the lifeless bodies of that species. Each had a strange quill stuck in its side, and the same quills dotted the trees that surrounded the habitat.

And then something in the shadows began to stir. Its shape wasn't recognizable as a dinosaur—at least, not as any known dinosaur.

The thing slowly unhinged its jaws and let out a long, tortured scream like no other.

CHAPTER SIX

"**W**e gotta fix that hole," Darius said. He didn't need to finish the sentence for the others to understand what he meant.

Kenji looked at Darius, his eyes getting brighter. "There is another dock not far from here," he said. "A private dock. The dock near my penthouse! There's a private pier and everything!"

Yasmina looked astonished. "And you're just *now* telling us this?"

"Um, kind of had other things on my mind. Like not dying," Kenji replied.

Darius's mind was already at work. "That penthouse could have everything we need."

"*Will* have everything we need," Kenji corrected him. "My dad loves boats. He's got all sorts of nautical junk."

Sammy smiled. "Well, then, let's go!"

The trip to Kenji's penthouse was surprisingly short, and it wasn't long before the kids found themselves docked at a pier in a secluded inlet ringed by thick jungle. Set back in the trees was a gleaming ten-story tower made of glass and steel.

"Welcome to the most exclusive spot on the island," Kenji said proudly.

They came to the end of the dock, arriving at a rack of scooters.

"It's only a short ride away," Kenji said with a smile.

Everyone hopped on a scooter save Ben, who climbed on Bumpy for the ride to the penthouse. Kenji led the way, clearly excited.

They were on the path to the penthouse when a Monolophosaurus burst out from the trees. The group shouted in surprise.

"You want me and Bumps to go back and . . . discourage it?" Ben asked.

"Nah," Darius said. "It's just a Monolophosaurus. They're loners—pretty much keep to themselves."

Darius watched as the Monolophosaurus looked around for a moment, then departed into the jungle.

"Then onward!" Kenji shouted. "Paradise awaits!"

They took off toward the penthouse.

If they had lingered for just another few seconds, they would have seen the Monolophosaurus slowly reemerge from the jungle.

And then another.

And another.

With no power on the island, the kids had to forego the elevator and walk up the ten flights of stairs. They were rewarded with the stunning view from Kenji's penthouse. There were huge windows all around, providing a spectacular look at the ocean and jungle.

"Welcome, friends, to Casa de Kenji," Kenji said.

Kenji watched as his friends looked at the penthouse, amazed. Yasmina found the kitchen and came back into the main room with an armful of chips, popcorn, and pretzels.

"Snacks!" she yelled, and handed out the bags to everyone.

"Hello?" Ben said impatiently. "I thought we were supposed to be searching for gas? A patch for the boat? A GPS? Any of this ringing a bell?"

"Dude, chill," Kenji said, and handed a bottle to Ben. "Have some water."

Down below, Bumpy waited for the others. She grazed in a stretch of grass, bending down, grabbing a mouthful, and happily munching away.

BANG!

Bumpy raised her head, suddenly alert. She looked around and saw two Monolophosauruses smashing their ridged snouts against a vent on the side of the penthouse.

CLANG!

The grate that covered the vent fell away, and the predators climbed inside.

"Something's up with Bumpy," Ben said as he watched the dinosaur bang her tail against the ground. "She only acts like that when she senses danger . . . or when she's constipated."

"I'm sure it's nothing," Kenji said reassuringly, enjoying the sense of *not* being in danger.

"We can't risk it," Darius said, moving away from the window. "Kenji, you said your dad has a portable GPS up here?"

"Yeah, somewhere," Kenji replied.

Ben was already moving. "I'll go down to the garage. If there's gas or something to patch the boat with, that's where it'll be."

"We're coming with," Yasmina said, pointing at herself and Sammy.

"Good plan," Darius said. "The sooner we find what we need, the sooner we get home."

Ben, Yasmina, and Sammy departed the main room, closing the door behind them.

And then the door creaked open. . . .

"Do you hear that? Ben said as they walked down the hallway toward the stairwell door. There was a strange sound, like scraping, coming from inside the stairwell. But as soon as it started, the scraping stopped.

Ben approached the door slowly and peered through the small window set into it.

BAM!

A Monolophosaurus slammed its head against the glass from the other side, and everyone jumped back, screaming.

BAM! BAM! BAM!

The Monolophosaurus kept at it, ramming its head into the door.

"Darius said they kept to themselves!" Sammy exclaimed.

"Back to the penthouse!" Ben said, and they ran

back down the hallway.

They froze in their tracks when they saw a shadow appear on the wall toward the other end of the hallway.

Another Monolophosaurus was coming their way . . . and it was closer to the penthouse door than they were!

Behind them, on the other side of the stairwell door, the first Monolophosaurus continued its assault, ramming the door.

Ahead, the shadow of the Monolophosaurus was looming closer and closer.

"Hey!" Sammy whispered. She pointed at an air-conditioning vent in the ceiling.

Not another word was spoken.

As the Monolophosaurus turned the corner in search of its prey, it found nothing. There was no one in the hallway at all. Only the grate from the air-conditioning vent dangled above.

Darius was searching Kenji's father's study when he saw something shiny and picked it up. "A compass! It's not a GPS, but it'll do."

They were interrupted by a CREAK . . . the sound of a door opening.

The kids ran for the door that led to the main room. It was now ajar, a hooked Monolophosaurus claw slowly pushing it open.

"What is that?" Kenji asked.

"Gonna take a wild guess and say 'dinosaur'!" Brooklynn replied.

The kids threw their weight against the door, trying to shut it, but the Monolophosaurus kept forcing it open. With a final push, they managed to shut the door, keeping the dinosaur out.

That was when the Monolophosaurus smashed through the door.

"That's impossible!" Kenji shouted.

"The elevator!" Brooklynn suggested.

"That's definitely not working!" Kenji replied.

"We can climb down through the shaft!" Darius suggested.

Darius and Brooklynn ran to the elevator doors, but Kenji hesitated.

BAM!

A large chunk of the door flew away as the Monolophosaurus thrust more of its body into the room.

"Kenji, come on!" Darius hollered as he and Brooklynn struggled to pry open the doors to the elevator shaft.

They managed to get them open, and taking

hold of the cables that stretched from floor to ceiling, started to lower themselves down the shaft.

As the Monolophosaurus tore another chunk of the door away, Kenji made a break for it. Running for the elevator shaft, he spied a small sculpture on a pedestal. Taking the sculpture, Kenji headed into the shaft and grabbed a cable. Lowering himself down, he heard the Monolophosaurus burst into the room and race over to the open elevator shaft! Kenji looked up and saw the dinosaur stop short, unable to follow.

A metal ceiling grate fell to the floor with a loud CLANG as Sammy, Ben, and Yasmina hit the bottom of the air vent.

Ben was dangling upside down, sticking his head through the open vent. There were no dinosaurs in sight, so he jumped down into the hallway, followed by Yasmina and Sammy. They walked by a door with a small sign with the numbers 401.

"Fourth floor," Yasmina said.

Cracking open the stairwell door, Ben looked inside.

"All clear," he said. "Stay sharp. They could be anywhere."

The three kids entered the stairwell, quietly

closing the heavy door behind them.

Luck seemed to be with them this time, as there wasn't a Monolophosaurus to be heard or seen in the stairwell. They made their way down the last four flights of stairs, and, opening the door at the bottom, found themselves in a huge, cavernous garage. It was mostly empty, with a supply closet on one side and four—FOUR!—stretch limousines.

"Limos on a jungle island," Ben said, shaking his head. "That's practical."

Sammy walked over to the supply closet and looked inside. There was a whole bunch of random stuff, like a garden hose and a tube of tire sealant.

"Anything useful in there, Sammy?" Yasmina asked. Then she spotted the tube of tire sealant and grabbed it. "Sealant! We could use this to patch the yacht!"

"Now all we need is gas. Where would they keep the gas?" Ben wondered.

The kids looked around the garage, and then, slowly, they all turned to stare at the four limousines.

Two Monolophosauruses snarled and snapped their jaws from the penthouse as they stared down the elevator shaft. Brooklynn was climbing down the cables, followed by Darius, and finally, Kenji.

BAM! BAM! BAM!

Brooklynn was startled at the sudden banging, which echoed throughout the elevator shaft.

"Where are they coming from?" she asked.

Before anyone could respond, a Monolophosaurus burst through a vent that led into the elevator shaft. The creature shrieked loudly, snapping its jaws. Then it swiped a hooked claw at them.

"Look out!" Darius warned. Twisting and swinging, the kids managed to avoid the Monolophosaurus's attacks.

CLANG!

A vent burst open on the other side of the shaft, and a second Monolophosaurus appeared.

"On your right!" Kenji shouted.

The Monolophosaurus pulled back and then jumped toward Darius! Twisting or swinging the cable wasn't going to work this time, so Darius loosened his grip on the line and slid down several feet, just clear of the dinosaur. The Monolophosaurus crashed into an air vent on the other side of the elevator shaft and struggled to pull itself up. Darius tightened his hands around the cable once more.

Brooklynn set down on top of the elevator car at the bottom of the shaft. She went to the hatch and tried to pop it open.

"It's stuck!" Brooklynn said.

Darius was right behind her. He joined Brooklynn in tugging at the hatch, but it wouldn't budge.

Looking up, Brooklynn noticed the closed elevator exit doors on the floor above them. They were just within reach.

"Come on!" she said as she and Darius started to pry open the exit doors. They managed to get them open and climb into the hallway.

Kenji slid to the roof of the elevator car. At that same moment, the Monolophosaurus that had been clinging to the air vent above lost its grip. It crashed onto the elevator car, next to him!

The dinosaur regained its footing, snapping at the boy. Without thinking, Kenji hit the dinosaur with his father's sculpture. Stunned, the Monolophosaurus stopped in its tracks. Kenji looked at the sculpture in his hands and saw that it was now broken in two.

The Monolophosaurus quickly recovered and lunged. Kenji hit the dinosaur again, letting go of the statue. It bought him just enough time to climb up to the doors above and enter the hallway.

Kenji had just made it up when Darius and Brooklynn let go of the elevator doors. They snapped closed right before the Monolophosaurus lunged at them.

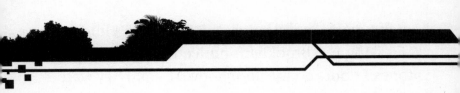

CHAPTER SEVEN

Ben and Yasmina were almost done siphoning gasoline from the limousines when they heard scraping sounds from the air vents.

Then there was a loud shriek as a Monolophosaurus jumped down from a grate in the ceiling. It was quickly followed by another. As the dinosaurs bore down on them, Ben tossed the hose aside and sealed the fuel can.

Yasmina opened the door to a limo, then shouted, "In here!"

The three kids jumped inside, and Ben shut the door.

WHAM!

A Monolophosaurus slammed into the vehicle.

WHAM!

"Let's go!" Yasmina said.

"How?" Ben asked. "We just took all the gas out of the limos!"

Sammy thought for a second, then pointed down the row of limousines to the one on the end. "Not that one," she said.

The kids got out of the car and raced across the garage with the Monolophosauruses behind them, jaws snapping. They opened the door to the last limo and were almost inside when another Monolophosaurus made a go at Yasmina's leg! Sammy managed to pull her into the car, avoiding the dinosaur. Then Yasmina turned around and kicked the creature as they slammed the door shut.

Yasmina then climbed into the driver's seat and was overjoyed to see the key in the ignition. She turned it, and the limo registered a full tank of gas. Right as she was about to pull out—THUMP!

A Monolophosaurus threw itself against the windshield, piercing the glass with its hooked claws!

Yasmina put the limo in reverse. It jerked backward, throwing the Monolophosaurus to the floor. Then she put the car in drive and headed for the garage exit.

Brooklynn, Darius, and Kenji had just exited the building when two Monolophosauruses tore through the door.

They heard the sound of a car engine and were

surprised to see a limousine barreling toward them! The limousine slowed down, and a door opened, revealing Sammy inside. The three jumped right in and shut the door.

Ben poked his head up through the limo's sunroof and yelled, "Let's hit it, Bumpy!"

At the sound of Ben's voice, Bumpy thrashed her tail at the dinosaurs, then ran off, following the limo.

The kids had made it back to the yacht, ahead of the Monolophosauruses. Maybe they wouldn't follow? At least, the campers *hoped* they wouldn't follow.

On the bridge of the yacht, Darius looked at the instrument panel. The red needle on the fuel gauge was now at FULL. Then he headed out to the pier, where he joined Ben and Brooklynn at the taped-up hole in the yacht's hull.

"How are we gonna fix this thing?" Darius asked as Sammy approached.

Kenji and Yasmina joined them, and they all started to offer ideas on how to repair the hull.

More duct tape was suggested, along with making a flame thrower. The duct tape made sense, the flame thrower less so.

A drone flew just over the water and headed into the jungle. It swooped between tree branches, searching . . . searching. Something darted in front of the drone's camera. It moved too fast to be identified.

The drone was beginning to turn around when a long, gnarled, misshapen claw swiped at it, and its camera went black.

"It ain't pretty, but it should be watertight," Brooklynn said.

The kids were gathered around the hole in the yacht's hull. Rather, where the hole used to be. Now there was a Camp Cretaceous cafeteria tray covering the spot, around which Brooklynn slathered tire sealant.

"Dope!" Kenji said. "Let's leave already!"

As everyone began to chatter about leaving Isla Nublar at last, Darius picked up the tube of tire sealant. "Hold up, guys. It says here we have to wait forty-eight hours for it to set."

Everyone groaned loudly and then settled in for the long wait.

As they surveyed the yacht, Sammy leaned over to Brooklynn.

"Can I talk to you a sec?" she whispered. "I need your help with something . . . personal."

"Girl, spill everything," Brooklynn said as she and Sammy walked off the dock onto the shore.

"Look, I was just thinkin' . . . since we've got two more days on the island, I wanna try and figure out why Mantah Corp sent me here. Maybe if I can find out what they're really up to, I can use that info against them and—"

"Say no more!" Brooklynn exclaimed. "Of course I'll help. It's gotta be related to E seven fifty. It was on Dr. Wu's computer, the envelope with the key card, that door on the monitors! It can't be a coincidence."

Sammy nodded as she pulled out a folded brochure. "Right! I've got some ideas on where to look. I found this island map at Kenji's condo. It's pretty old, but—"

"Come on, we'll take the gyrosphere," Brooklynn said.

"Be back later, Kenji!" Sammy called out as they jogged past him. "We're gonna go investigate a mystery!"

"What's new?" Kenji said as the girls disappeared.

He looked at the compass until he was distracted by the high-pitched sound of an approaching Compsognathus.

"Ugh, get outta here!" Yasmina said.

"I got this," Kenji stated as he dug into his pocket and produced a shiny coin. "Grabbed some quarters from the penthouse. Best way to keep the Compys away."

He threw the coin over the Compy's head. It landed on the ground, sparkling in the sun. Kenji and Yasmina watched as the dinosaur ran after the quarter.

"Not so sure that's a good idea," Darius said. "You know what you get when you feed a pigeon. . . ."

"More pigeons," Yasmina said, answering for Kenji. Three more Compys appeared.

"Then it's a good thing I'm rich!" Kenji said. He set the compass down on a rock, and pulled more quarters out of his pockets and threw them. The Compys took off after the coins.

Yasmina and Darius rolled their eyes. Behind them, another Compsognathus scurried up, attracted by the sun glinting off the shiny compass. The Compy picked it up in its mouth and ran to the edge of the jungle.

"Without that compass, we're stuck on the island!" Darius whispered. "Just approach her slowly. . . ."

At the sound of Darius's voice, the Compy cocked its head. Then it ran off with the compass.

Darius, Kenji, and Yasmina passed Ben and Bumpy, who came out of the jungle.

"Be back later, Ben! You're in charge!" Kenji yelled.

Ben watched them run off after the Compy, shrugging his shoulders.

"Anyone see where it went?" Yasmina asked. Darius and Kenji were right behind her. All around them, the jungle was thicker than anything they'd yet encountered.

As they walked forward, Darius saw something on a hillside—a battered old 4x4.

"Darius!" Yasmina shouted.

Darius joined Yasmina and Kenji. A second later, two glowing eyes appeared from within the dark foliage, staring at Darius as he walked away.

The kids could hear the Compy, but it wasn't close.

"I think it's coming from over there," Darius said.

They kept walking, Kenji's and Yasmina's eyes glued to the jungle, looking for the Compy. At last, Darius looked up, and his jaw practically hit the ground.

"Guys, do you know where we are?" he said, his voice growing louder.

They were standing in front of two huge doors covered in thick jungle vines.

Darius knew these doors. He had seen them before in his video game and in books.

"Welcome to Jurassic Park," he said.

CHAPTER EIGHT

"This is where it all began! I can't believe we're actually here," Darius said as they walked toward the Jurassic Park Visitor Center. The whole area had been reclaimed by nature. Plants had grown over the buildings and obscured the road that led to them.

Suddenly, a Compsognathus darted past them and through the front doors of the Visitor Center.

"A Compy! Maybe the others went in there, too," Darius said. He and Yasmina followed it, a reluctant Kenji tagging along.

The inside of the Visitor Center didn't look any more inviting than the outside. The place was completely run-down, with scaffolding and vines hanging from the ceiling. Peeking out from the foliage was the skeleton of a T. rex. Murals of Velociraptors lined the walls.

Kenji shuddered.

There was a scuttling sound, and everyone reacted. Darius pointed to the ceiling, where Compys clung to the beams. They were gnawing on the metal, trying to get at the nuts and bolts. Darius watched as one particular Compy walked along a beam above, toward what appeared to be some kind of nest in the ceiling.

"Look!" Darius said, pointing above as he saw the gleam of the compass in the Compy's mouth. "We gotta get up there."

"C'mon, guys, like this! Yasmina said.

They had spent what seemed like an hour pushing the heavy vending machine along the floor to the middle of the room. It was now right beneath the old scaffolding. With ease, Yasmina climbed atop the vending machine, then grabbed a vine hanging from the scaffolding. In a flash, she was on the scaffolding itself. The metal creaked, and Yasmina pulled on it a few times to make sure it was safe. Then she nodded for Darius and Kenji to join her.

Yasmina had her eyes on the compass as she moved. She reached for a handhold, and a Compsognathus popped up, hissing at her, snapping at her hand. Pulling her hand back, she said, "Watch out for the Compys."

Darius and Kenji had now made it to the scaffolding and were inching their way forward. Beneath them, there came a low growl. A sound that was distinctly *not* coming from a Compsognathus.

Above them, the Compys came to attention and looked down. The kids joined them in looking. A shadow crossed the floor. It was a Velociraptor. It had a thick blue stripe along its side.

Darius put his finger to his lips, indicating the need for quiet. Kenji and Yasmina nodded, frozen in place. They watched as the Velociraptor warily stalked across the room. It was obviously on the hunt.

Yasmina heard a rustling sound above and saw two Compys fighting over the compass. They were nudging it back and forth, and it was nearing the edge of the nest. What if it fell? Yasmina couldn't let that happen. She climbed ahead as quietly as possible.

As she grew closer, the compass seemed to get closer to the edge, closer to falling. Darius and Kenji watched.

The blue Velociraptor continued to pace below.

Yasmina was very nearly in the nest and just about to grab the compass when it fell. The shiny object was heading directly for the Velociraptor's head!

But before the compass could hit the creature,

Darius shot his hand out, catching it. The soft thump of the object landing in Darius's hand was loud enough that the Velociraptor cocked its head and listened. Then it slowly walked toward the vending machine.

And the Velociraptor jumped!

The kids shuddered, but the Velociraptor had not appeared on top of the vending machine. Instead, the dinosaur emerged from behind it, with a lifeless Compsognathus in its jaws. Satisfied, it turned and left the Visitor Center.

A few moments later, the kids had climbed back down. Darius looked at the Velociraptor murals that lined the walls, and shook his head. "That's one of the Raptors we saw the first night at camp," he said. "Must be nesting in here now."

"Love what it's done with the place, but let's get outta here before it comes back," Yasmina suggested.

They started toward the exit but froze in their tracks as one of the Raptor murals began to move!

Except it wasn't a mural. It was the blue Velociraptor standing in front of the mural. The dinosaur had only pretended to leave!

"Clever guy," Kenji said, his feet rooted to the floor in fear.

"Girl . . . She's a girl," Darius corrected his friend. Kenji rolled his eyes.

"So, what do we do now?" Kenji asked.

The blue Velociraptor was now staring at the kids. The dinosaur snarled at them.

"Run?" Yasmina offered.

A moment later, Yasmina, Darius, and Kenji sprinted out of the Visitor Center and down the front steps. The nimble blue Velociraptor followed.

"Up there!" Darius shouted, pointing at the abandoned 4x4 he had spotted earlier. "The car!"

They made it to the vehicle, yanked open the doors, and hopped inside. Kenji was in the driver's seat, and Yasmina was riding shotgun.

In the seat behind them, Darius shouted, "Start the engine!"

There was a key in the ignition, and Kenji quickly turned it.

Nothing.

Kenji tried it again, but it still wouldn't start.

Looking around, Darius saw a tranquilizer rifle next to him. "Maybe we can—"

WHAM!

The blue Velociraptor had reached the vehicle, smashing into its side.

WHAM!

WHAM!

Then the banging suddenly stopped, and the blue Velociraptor wasn't there.

"Where'd she go?" Yasmina wondered.

"Maybe she went back to get her Raptor friends," Kenji said.

"If she still had a pack, they'd be here by now," Darius said. "She's alone."

BAM!

The kids were startled by the loud noise and jostling of the vehicle when the blue Velociraptor jumped onto the hood!

Unable to start the vehicle, Kenji had another idea. He released the parking brake, and as the dinosaur tried to smash through the window, the 4x4 started to roll down the hill.

Kenji did his best to guide the vehicle, but it was nearly impossible without power steering and with a dinosaur pounding away at the windshield.

The 4x4 picked up more speed until it reached the bottom of the hill and its momentum caused the vehicle to flip over, landing on the roof.

"Where is she?" Yasmina said, looking around. "Do you see her?"

Kenji rubbed his head. "I'm fine. Thanks for asking."

Then they heard it. Something soft that sounded

like the Velociraptor, but the noise was weak. Like a cry.

"Come on," Darius said as he kicked open the door, tranquilizer rifle in hand.

Everyone crawled out of the overturned vehicle, and then they saw her. The blue Velociraptor was stuck beneath the 4x4.

"She's trapped," Darius said.

"Lucky us—let's go!" Kenji replied.

Kenji and Yasmina turned to leave, but Darius was rooted to the spot. He couldn't take his eyes off the dinosaur. Suddenly, there was a familiar high-pitched sound, and out from the jungle stepped a Compsognathus.

The Compy approached the trapped Velociraptor, curious. Then another Compy emerged from the jungle, followed by another. Slowly, the injured dinosaur was surrounded by Compys.

"C'mon, man, we gotta go!" Kenji said.

"They'll kill her, eat her alive," Darius said.

"Not our problem, bro. Enemy of my enemy and all that."

Yasmina looked at Darius, tilting her head slightly. "But she wasn't our enemy. We were trespassing in her home."

Kenji desperately wanted to leave but knew that Darius was right. "Okay, fine, dino whisperer. What do we do?"

"We gotta distract the Compys," Darius said.

Immediately, Kenji's eyes lit up, and he took off running.

Yasmina and Darius had no idea where Kenji was headed but figured he must have some brilliant idea. That left them to keep the Compys away until Kenji returned. They took turns swinging the tranquilizer rifle, trying to keep the tiny dinosaurs at bay.

"Shoo! Get back!" Darius shouted.

"Get outta here!" Yasmina yelled.

The Compys were getting closer to the blue Velociraptor when, suddenly, there was the tinny CLANG of something small and metallic hitting the old 4x4.

Then another CLANG.

And another.

This caught the Compys' attention, and they looked up. There was Kenji, with a big handful of coins.

"You like that? More where that came from!" Kenji said, and then he chucked the handful of coins into the jungle. Instantly, the Compys forgot about the Velociraptor and took off into the jungle after the shiny coins.

"Kenji for the win!" Yasmina cried out.

Darius realized that Kenji had run back to the Visitor Center, cracked open the dilapidated vending machine, and removed the quarters!

Kenji's stunt bought them a little time. The three kids took positions around the 4x4 and started to lift the vehicle off the blue Velociraptor. Darius looked at the dinosaur, making eye contact with her. The dinosaur seemed calm, like she almost understood what Darius was trying to do.

With all their might, the kids kept the vehicle off the Velociraptor as she wriggled free. Unable to hold the 4x4 any longer, they let go. Darius grabbed the tranquilizer as the blue Velociraptor locked eyes with Darius.

They stared at one another for a moment, then Darius calmly, deliberately put the tranquilizer rifle on the ground. Then he slowly put his arms out wide.

"Trust me."

The blue Velociraptor looked at Yasmina and Kenji, then back at Darius. She could have pounced on them if she had wanted to, but she didn't.

"Back up slowly," Darius said. "And whatever you do, don't turn your back."

As they started to leave, Darius was horrified as a shiny quarter hit the blue Velociraptor right in the chest, bouncing off. He shot Kenji a look. Kenji shrugged—he had thrown the quarter, trying to distract the dinosaur!

In response, the blue Velociraptor snarled.

"Never mind! Go!" Darius cried, and the dinosaur snarled again as the kids sprinted away.

"Well, it doesn't look under construction, does it?" Brooklynn said.

She and Sammy had just stepped out of the gyrosphere, in front of a boring, nondescript building with a big sign that said UNDER CONSTRUCTION.

The girls looked at each other, a little worried, and then entered the building.

Inside, they walked down a long, dark hallway. At the end was a door that was hanging from its hinges, like it had been ripped open.

A thin shift of light illuminated the door, and the girls could make out a small sign that read E-750.

They walked inside and found themselves in a thoroughly trashed laboratory. Sammy walked by a row of test tubes as Brooklynn opened a laptop. Surprisingly, it still had battery power, and the screen came on.

"Video files!" Brooklynn said as she pointed to folders on the screen.

Sammy smiled as she clicked on a folder and opened a video file.

Dr. Wu appeared on-screen, standing in the same lab that Sammy and Brooklynn were in.

"I am delighted to announce that the E seven fifty project is a complete success!" Dr. Wu said to the camera. "I have created the world's first hybrid dinosaur—the Scorpios rex!"

Then something shrieked behind Dr. Wu. "Granted, its appearance and behavior are a bit . . . unusual. But I know Mr. Masrani will be pleased."

There was a cut in the video, then it resumed with the next entry.

But Dr. Wu was no longer smiling. "Mr. Masrani was *not* pleased. He called Scorpios 'too ugly to put on display.' Still, despite his . . . shortsightedness, I shall continue my work, undeterred."

Sammy and Brooklynn looked at each other, worried.

The next entry began. Dr. Wu now seemed agitated. "The Scorpios rex's mind has turned out to be as fragmented and unpredictable as its body," he said. "One moment placid, the next . . . extremely aggressive."

Suddenly, the video cut off, and when it resumed, there was chaos. Scientists were running around, crowding Dr. Wu, who was now sprawled on the floor.

"Dr. Wu is down!" a scientist cried out.

"Antidote! Antidote!" another shouted.

A technician ran past the camera, holding what

appeared to be a quill. Then a scientist with a hypo-
dermic needle filled with a red fluid ran toward Dr.
Wu, and the video cut once more.

When it resumed, Dr. Wu was sitting in a chair,
breathing hard. He seemed scared. "After the . . .
accident, Mr. Masrani ordered me to destroy the
specimen. And yet, I can't bring myself to end this
important research."

The camera followed Dr. Wu as he walked toward a large cylindrical glass case. There was clearly
something huge inside.

"I've decided to put the Scorpios into cryogenic
suspension indefinitely, until I can determine what
exactly went wrong."

"Did ya see how scared he was?" Sammy asked
when the video ended.

"Yeah," Brooklynn replied. "If the Indominus
rex was a 'success,' what kind of crazy scary was a
failure like the Scorpios rex?"

"Good thing he froze it," Sammy said. But her
friend didn't say anything. "Brooklynn?"

She saw Brooklynn was looking at a dark corner
of the lab. Sammy followed her eyes, and they saw
it. The shattered remains of a large glass cylinder.

It was the same cylinder from the video, the one
that contained the Scorpios Rex.

CHAPTER NINE

"**W**e gotta warn the others," Brooklynn said as they raced from Dr. Wu's secret lab toward their gyrosphere.

But before they could reach their vehicle, a pack of dinosaurs exploded from the jungle! Ceratosauruses, Ankylosauruses, Monolophosauruses, and more came running, and the girls barely had time to duck behind a rock to avoid being trampled.

WHAM!

One of the dinosaurs kicked the gyrosphere, sending it crashing into a tall tree, and smoke began to pour out.

Brooklynn and Sammy peeked around the rock, watching the dinosaurs as they ran away.

"Why are they running at us?" Sammy asked.

"Because they're running from something else," Brooklynn said gravely. "Come on."

Kenji, Darius, Yasmina, and Ben had returned to Camp Cretaceous to gather last-minute supplies they would need for their ocean voyage. Kenji climbed the ladder leading to the second floor of their fort, expecting to see Darius, but there was no sign of the dinosaur-obsessed kid. Then he looked at the makeshift chalkboard and saw a message:

> Kenji—
>   Gotta go take care of something for a bit . . . leaving you in charge while I'm gone . . . know you can handle it. Can you pack all the supplies we need for our trip? . . . Channel 6 in case of emergency.

"*Pffft,*" Kenji said. "Easy. Captain Kenji is on it."

Happy to be in charge, Kenji did a little dance, unaware that Ben was watching him.

Kenji coughed, then said, "I'm in charge. I need you to pack . . . toilet paper."

"Seriously?" Ben asked.

"We're gonna need it on the way to Costa Rica, and . . . I'm in charge!"

Ben shrugged his shoulders and said, "Sure," then headed off in pursuit of toilet paper.

While the others gathered supplies, Darius made his way out to some tall grass. There, he stood in awe as he watched a flock of Gallimimuses race through the plants. They would come to a stop, then peck at the ground like some kind of prehistoric ostriches.

Darius's dad had loved the Gallimimuses. Darius had sworn that there was no way he was going to leave Isla Nublar without seeing them. He owed his dad that much.

Darius couldn't take his eyes off the dinosaurs! And apparently, one of the Gallimimuses couldn't take her eyes off Darius, either. The dinosaur noticed him and took a step closer to Darius. Then another. Their eyes met, and Darius couldn't believe his good fortune.

Then the radio crackled, and the Gallimimus stopped approaching.

"Captain Kenji to Dariusaurus," came the voice over the radio.

Darius picked up the radio. "Go for Dariusaurus."

"You're sure that's the call sign you want?" Kenji asked.

"Didja need something?" Darius asked, a little impatient.

"Uh . . . yep! Just wanted to let you know that I've got this whole 'in charge' thing on lock."

"I know, man," Darius said sincerely. "I believe in you."

They signed off, and Darius put the radio in his pocket.

Back at camp, Kenji and Yasmina had started to gather supplies.

"Ben should be helping, but I sent him to get toilet paper like an hour ago and he hasn't come back," Kenji said, frustrated.

"An hour?" Yasmina said. "To get something from just over there?" She pointed across the way.

"Oh," Kenji said as it slowly dawned on him. "Do you think something happened to him?"

"On *this* island? I think it's a distinct possibility!"

The two looked at each other for a moment and then went off in search of Ben.

"Good girl," Darius said as he slowly approached

the Gallimimus. The dinosaur was wary of him but didn't move as Darius extended his hand, a clump of grass in his palm. Then the Gallimimus sniffed the grass and gently pecked at it.

Crackling static from the radio made the Gallimimus back away. Then it turned and trotted back to the flock.

"What's up, Captain Kenji?" Darius said, trying to sound like he wasn't disappointed.

"What would you do if . . . a totally capable but scrawny *dinosaur* went missing?" Kenji said.

"Huh?" Darius said. He thought Kenji's wording was really strange, especially the way he said "dinosaur" like he didn't really mean "dinosaur."

"Nothing—never mind. Don't worry about it," Kenji said quickly.

"Are you *sure*?" Darius asked.

"Absolutely!" Kenji said. "I got this."

Darius put the radio away, then thought for a moment. He pulled the radio back out and turned it off. He kept on walking, anxious to follow the Gallimimus flock. He saw them by the edge of the jungle.

But instead of their usual flock behavior, Darius was surprised to see the Gallimimuses were nestled in the tall grass . . . as if they were *hiding*.

Making his way to the tree line, Darius saw what looked like quills lodged in a tree trunk. He heard a creaking sound from above and tilted his head.

There was the limp body of a Gallimimus hanging in the branches.

"How . . . *what* did this?" Darius gasped.

"Ben! What the heck, man?!" Kenji said, raising his voice in anger.

They had found Ben and Bumpy in the grassland, where an Ankylosaurus herd was resting.

"I told you to get toilet paper!" Kenji said, irritated.

"And I did," Ben replied, and he pointed to a nearby bag filled with rolls of toilet paper. "Then I came to check on her." He patted Bumpy on the head, oblivious that his friends were upset with him.

"Kinda messed up that you took off and didn't tell anyone where you were going," Yasmina said.

"I didn't realize I needed to ask permission to live my life," Ben shot back.

"It's not about that!" Kenji said. "It's about being a team player. Darius asked us to get supplies for everyone, and instead, we had to go looking for you! Are you part of this team or not?"

Ben glared at Kenji, then said, "Okay, sheesh. I'm part of the team." He picked up the bag of toilet paper and threw it at Kenji. "For the next couple of days, anyway."

"What are you talking about?" Yasmina asked.

"After we go home, it's not like any of us will ever see each other again," Ben said. Then he turned to Bumpy, and the two walked away, heading back for camp.

Above them, dark gray storm clouds moved in, and thunder rumbled.

"What kind of dinosaur kills, then drags its victim up into a tree?" Darius asked aloud. "This doesn't make sense."

Then he heard something rustling behind a thick cluster of foliage. He squinted hard—what was that shape? Was it watching him? What was it?

Darius leaned in, and when he swallowed, he felt a lump in his throat.

Suddenly, Brooklynn and Sammy burst from the trees, and Darius felt like he was going to jump out of his skin.

"Oh my gosh, Darius, we—we saw this thing in Wu's lab!" Brooklynn said. "He called it his first hybrid. The, uh, the Scorpios rex! It's, like, the pre-Indominus rex."

"But way more dangerous and unpredictable and unstable!" Sammy said.

Darius looked around them and stared at the

Gallimimus in the tree. "All the strange dino behavior we've seen . . . the quills . . . and that Gallimimus . . . This Scorpios isn't like anything we've ever encountered. It's disrupted the entire ecosystem of the island, which means—"

"—we're in more danger than we ever have been," Sammy said, completing his sentence.

"We can't wait any longer," Brooklynn said with urgency. "We have to leave the island. Now."

"Phew," Kenji said as he raced back into camp. "Darius isn't back yet. We still have time."

Ben, Bumpy, and Yasmina followed him.

"All right. We still need food and water," Kenji said.

CRACKLE!

The radio came to life, and Kenji removed it from his pocket.

"Kenji!" Darius said, his voice full of panic. "We have to get out of here right now!"

Kenji looked at Ben and Yasmina, confused. "What? What are you—"

"There's another hybrid dinosaur!" Brooklynn said.

Kenji gulped as he looked back at the campground. They hadn't put anything together yet. No food, no water, no nothing. Well, except for toilet paper.

Then he took a deep breath, grabbed the radio from Yasmina, and said, "Yaz will go ahead to the boat and get it ready for launch. Ben and I will pack up the essentials. Darius, Brooklynn, Sammy—swing by camp to help us carry everything."

"Copy that," Darius said. "See you soon."

Without saying a word, Yasmina sprinted off into the jungle, heading for the yacht. Ben and Kenji started to gather the supplies as a crack of thunder echoed through the camp. The storm clouds opened up, and it started to pour.

"The surf is way too intense to cast off," Yasmina said, panting from running to the dock and back so quickly. "Boat's already taking on water. No way to leave till the seas calm down."

Darius looked at Sammy and Brooklynn, who dropped their supplies.

"What's the big deal?" Yasmina said. "We hide out until the storm breaks, right?"

"Yeah, avoiding killer dinos is kind of our thing," Kenji said glibly.

"We've only survived this long because we know

how dinosaurs should act," Darius said. "With the Scorpios rex on a rampage, all bets are off. Total chaos. Soon, survival will be impossible."

Darius was just about to say something else when the ground began to shake. Puddles vibrated, and everyone felt their legs wobble.

Suddenly, dinosaurs of all kinds filled the camp, running right through it. They were bellowing, grunting, hissing—all the sounds dinosaurs made when frightened. Bumpy must have sensed it, too, because she took off with the rest of the herd!

"Bumpy!" Ben shouted loudly as the ground shook again.

CHAPTER TEN

"**W**e gotta keep that thing out!" Darius said as the rain continued to pour down.

Kenji pointed at a nearby pile of debris. "We could use some of the rubble to fortify the fence? Maybe?"

"Yeah, that works!" Darius said, and the group spread out in search of anything they could possibly use to reinforce the fence against the hybrid.

A little ways off, Yasmina was tugging on a wooden board, trying to free it from a pile of wreckage.

"Hey, Yaz?" Sammy said, running up to her.

Yasmina stopped what she was doing and looked at Sammy.

There was an awkward pause, and Sammy suddenly started to speak . . . and she didn't stop. "I've been trying to find a good time to tell you this, and, well, being hunted by an especially murderous dinosaur really puts things into perspective, and

I'm rambling now so I'm just gonna say it. You're my best friend, Yaz, and I'm really glad we got to know each other even if it *was* because of the, ya know, murderous dinosaurs."

"Sammy, I . . . ," Yasmina started. Then, "But Ben's right. When we get off this island, you're gonna go back to Texas, and I'll go back to training all the time. How is that gonna work? A random text or five-minute phone call at one a.m. isn't friendship. What's the point of having a best friend if you never even get to see each other? I'm sorry."

Then Yasmina turned away so Sammy couldn't see her crying.

Kenji and Darius removed the battery from an overturned 6x4 and hooked it up to the fence that encircled the camp. Now electrified, the fence sizzled raindrops upon impact.

Grabbing whatever weapons they could find, the kids climbed up the ladder to their fort. With their backs to each other, they formed a tight circle, scanning the outside for any signs of the approaching hybrid.

They didn't have to wait long.

As the lightning flashed, Darius caught a glimpse of something on the other side of the fence.

Something horrifying.

The creature was skinny, almost impossibly so for its size. Quills ran down its thick spine, and the sound of its heavy, labored breathing filled the camp over the sound of the rain. The monster seemed to be staring right at them.

Then, without warning, the hybrid charged right at the electrified fence. The creature was fast but awkward, clumsy. . . . It moved more like some kind of reanimated zombie than a living thing. It threw its entire body against the fence, receiving a terrible shock.

"Yes!" Kenji shouted.

They watched in terror as the hybrid paced along the fence, frustrated. There was another blinding flash of lightning, and when the kids looked down, the hybrid was gone.

They were so focused on the fence that none of them noticed that the hybrid was climbing a tree. The creature dropped down into the campground with a quiet thud.

Darius heard the sound and slowly turned his head as the hybrid stalked right for them.

"Run," Darius said.

They scrambled down the ladder as the hybrid charged their way. Its jaws were wide open, ready for a meal. Splitting up, Yasmina and Sammy went to the right, while the others headed left. The hybrid was now in the middle, between the kids.

The creature whipped around, chasing after Darius, Kenji, Ben, and Brooklynn. They were now at the other side of the camp, frantically trying to loosen boards from the fence. They managed to pry one off, but it accidentally hit the fence, showering them with sparks.

The hybrid slowed to a walk as if it knew the kids had nowhere else to go.

"They're trapped!" Yasmina shouted.

"The battery!" Sammy said as she raced over to the battery and the cables that connected it to the fence. Yasmina followed her, but it looked like they were too late. Even if they got to the battery, the hybrid was already close to their friends!

Darius, Brooklynn, Kenji, and Ben cowered and closed their eyes.

The hybrid was breathing harder, only inches away.

And then the lightning struck.

The bolt sliced through a huge tree, sending it crashing right into the fence on the opposite side of camp. The fence exploded, and the hybrid stopped in its tracks, rushing over to investigate, staring at the ball of flame that erupted into the air.

But the hybrid was only distracted for a moment.

It turned to face the kids once more. It took one step . . . then cocked its head, like it heard something in the distance. Suddenly, the hybrid jumped over the fence, ignoring the kids completely!

All at once, Darius, Brooklynn, Kenji, and Ben let out a deep breath. Sammy and Yasmina rushed over to their friends.

"Why did it leave?" Yasmina wondered.

"Not sure," Darius said, still trying to catch his breath. "Maybe it heard something it wanted more than us."

"That thing was . . . ," Sammy started, but then she stopped talking.

"Sammy, are you okay?" Darius asked.

Sammy gave Darius a curious look as she glanced down at her abdomen . . . and the quills that were stuck there. She gave him a weak smile, then collapsed on the ground.

A light rain was falling as the kids watched over Sammy. They had removed the quills from her, but Sammy was still unconscious. Brooklynn and Darius crouched down beside her as Yasmina held Sammy's hand.

Suddenly, Sammy's eyelids began to move, just a little, and she started to open them.

"Sammy, we're here. Everything's going to be okay," Yasmina said, her voice tinged with guilt. She was still upset over the harsh way she had spoken to Sammy earlier.

"Taking out the quills wasn't enough," Darius said. "The poison's already in her system. She needs an antidote."

Brooklynn jumped up. "The video in Wu's old lab! Sammy and I saw it! He was attacked by the Scorpios, and—and—and—they were giving him this, this shot from a red vial!"

Yasmina stood up and grabbed Brooklynn by the shoulders. "Where is this lab?"

Reaching into her pocket, Brooklynn took out a map and gave it to Yasmina. She pointed right at the location of the lab. Yasmina stared at the spot like she was memorizing it. Then she put the map into her sock.

"Take care of Sammy until I get back," she said, turning to leave camp.

"Go," Darius said. "We'll figure out a way to keep the Scorpios off your back."

Yasmina gave a sharp nod and ran off into the night.

"Okay, think! What do we know about this dinosaur so far?" Darius asked.

Kenji held up his hand like he was counting with his fingers. "It's straight-up terrifying. It climbs.

Breathes like a pug with a cold. And it moves weird."
Then Kenji started to mimic the hybrid's strange,
herky-jerky zombie-like movements.

"Yeah, but when that explosion went off . . . ,"
Brooklynn said.

"It didn't run from it. It went *toward* it," Darius
said, nodding. "Almost like it was hypnotized for a
sec . . . That's how we'll clear a path for Yaz!"

"I'm in," Ben said as he collected sticks and
spears to use as weapons.

Darius looked at the fallen Sammy and then to
Brooklynn and Kenji. He was clearly worried, and
Kenji nodded at his friend. "We'll take care of her,
bro," Kenji said. "Go kick some Scorpios butt for us."

The rain had stopped completely, but the wind had
yet to die down. Yasmina ran past the trees, ducking
swaying branches, moving as fast as she could. She
heard something rustling in the foliage up ahead,
and she took a deep breath.

"Hang on, Sammy," Yasmina said softly. "Just
hang on."

Then she skidded to a halt.

In front of her was a gushing river, the rough
waters churning from the heavy rain. The current
was moving swiftly; if she tried to swim across,

she'd be swept away. The path was blocked.

Yasmina looked around to see if there was some way around the river, but there didn't appear to be any. So she backed up and sprinted for the river. Before she could jump, Yasmina stumbled, falling into the water with a splash. The current carried her away!

Yasmina thrashed as she bobbed up and down in the water, trying to keep her head above the surface of the raging river. The current was taking her farther and farther away from her path! Yasmina remembered the map, and her heart sunk when she saw the map floating away from her—it must have fallen out of her sock.

"No!" she screamed, but it was useless.

Yasmina was drenched when she freed herself from the river. She had no idea where she was. Leaning against a tree, tired, she closed her eyes for a moment and thought of Sammy.

Since Yasmina arrived on the island, Sammy had tried to crack Yasmina's shell, to get to know her. At first, Yasmina resisted. But she couldn't help liking Sammy, and over time, she found that Sammy really *was* an amazing friend.

Determined, Yasmina stood up. Maybe she

could run back? Then she looked the other way and saw a sign featuring different Park attractions—their distance and direction.

Yasmina smiled as she read RAPTOR PADDOCK. She remembered seeing that on the map . . . and it was right near the lab!

She headed toward the Raptor paddock, knowing the hybrid was out there, somewhere.

CHAPTER ELEVEN

Brooklynn took Sammy's hand. "Can you hear me? I need you to hurry up and get better, okay?"

Kenji approached with a jug of water, setting it at Brooklynn's feet, along with a washcloth. Then he moved away quickly.

"You can come closer, you know," she said. "She's not contagious."

"Nah," Kenji said, shaking his head. "You look like you got things on lock, so I'm just . . . gonna not."

Brooklynn gave Sammy some water, then slowly walked over to Kenji. "It's okay. I'm scared, too," she said.

"I'm not scared," Kenji protested. "I mean, I am. I just . . . What if she . . . None of my friends have ever—"

"Don't say it," Brooklynn said. "Yaz is going to

come back with the antidote, and then everything will be fine."

As Yasmina neared the Raptor paddock, she heard shrieking. She recognized it immediately—it was the hybrid. On instinct, she stopped running and stayed in place, still as a statue.

Then she took a deep breath and cautiously approached the Raptor paddock. Ahead, she saw a nondescript building with a sign that said UNDER CONSTRUCTION.

As she drew nearer, her heart sank as she saw that several trees blocked the entrance.

"Oh, come on," Yasmina groaned.

Scrambling over a tree, she jumped to the other side. She pulled the door, but a tree prevented her from opening it more than a few inches. So she put her back against the door, placed her feet on the tree, and started to push. At last, she moved the tree just enough so that she could squeeze inside.

"There!" Ben said as he darted inside a dense grove of trees. He rummaged around the roots of an enormous tree and pulled out what looked like a full can of . . .

"Gasoline?" Darius asked. "Dude, how much did you take?"

"Not much," Ben said. "I figure we had plenty to get to Costa Rica, so I stashed some away. Ya know, in case of a rainy day."

Darius shook his head and said, "Ben, you beautiful, disturbed, beautiful boy."

"It has to be here!" Yasmina said frantically as she opened a cabinet, searching for the antidote.

But no matter how many cabinets she opened, she couldn't find anything.

Screaming in frustration, she overturned a desk, then pushed a chair. The chair sailed over to a wall, and Yasmina noticed that there was a first aid kit hanging there.

It can't be that easy, she thought. *Can it?*

Yasmina opened the kit. Inside was a red vial with the words E-750 ANTIDOTE written on it. Grabbing the vial and a few syringes, Yasmina sprinted out of the lab.

"We gotta hurry," Darius said.

He and Ben had made their way to the top of Lookout Point. Ben had the can of gasoline and was setting up a long fuse.

"I saw Yaz through the binoculars," Darius continued. "The Scorpios isn't far behind her."

Darius hopped into the gondola that was waiting, holding the other end of the fuse that connected to the can of gasoline. Ben was at the main control panel of the loading platform. He flipped a switch, and the gondola began to move. Ben jumped into the gondola as Darius unfurled the fuse.

Yasmina was running flat out when she heard the gut-wrenching shriek of the hybrid, and she instinctively covered her ears, dropping the vials!

"No, no, no, no!" she shouted as she reached down to pick them up. Then she saw the twisted, misshapen form of the hybrid coming closer.

"All right," Darius said. "Light it up."

Ben lit the fuse as the gondola descended from the top of Lookout Point. They watched as the fuse sparked and burned upward.

Yasmina locked eyes with the hybrid as she stuffed the vials into her pockets. The creature was watching her every move, waiting for the right time to strike.

But Yasmina wasn't going to wait. She took off in a sprint.

The hybrid followed, lumbering through trees. It opened its mouth, baring its sharp teeth, growling.

Yasmina had a lead over the hybrid. When she came to the river, the one that had swept her away before, she reached up, grabbed a vine hanging overhead, and swung over!

She turned to see the hybrid approach the river, momentarily puzzled. Then it scrambled up a tree—Yasmina realized it was going to do what it did back at the camp and climb a tree to jump over the river.

As the hybrid reached the top of the tree, Yasmina got to her feet. Then the hybrid fell from the tree and landed right near her!

Yasmina was afraid. Afraid she wouldn't make it back to Sammy with the antidote. Afraid to meet her end this way. And then that fear turned into anger.

"Go ahead, then!" she screamed. "Ya gonna do something, then do it already!"

But before the hybrid could strike, the world exploded. A giant fireball filled the sky, and the jungle shook. The hybrid whipped its head away from Yasmina and saw the bright explosion against the night sky. It cocked its head, then hurried away.

Yasmina couldn't believe it. She thought for sure she was done—but since she wasn't, she ran.

From the base of the mountain, Darius and Ben watched the explosion atop Lookout Point.

"Let's just hope it helped Yaz," Ben said.

They stared at it for another moment as Darius said, "Come on. We need to get back."

They took off into the jungle.

Yasmina had no idea how long she had been running. Minutes? An hour? Her body had been on autopilot, her mind focused on one thing and one thing only—making it to Sammy.

Up ahead, she saw . . . Was it the camp?

She saw the others yelling but couldn't make out the words. The sound of her own heartbeat pounded in her ears, drowning out all noise.

Yasmina's feet carried her into camp, where she

Darius and his friends think they are finally going to escape Jurassic World and get back home . . .

. . . but they quickly find out that building a seaworthy raft is a lot harder than it seems.

Even though the others are disheartened to be back on the island, Ben and Bumpy are happy to be reunited.

Darius senses that something is wrong with Ben, but it's not easy getting him to talk about what is bothering him.

The kids don't realize that they are being stalked by a predator—and the predator doesn't realize that it is being stalked by something even more dangerous!

While searching for hang glider sails at the top of a mountain, the kids discover that it is not wise to upset a Dimorphodon nest.

Brooklynn and Yasmina make a quick getaway with one of the hang gliders.

Unfortunately, the entire colony of Dimorphodons comes after them.

The Dimorphondons attack Sammy and Kenji in the Sky Gondola as well.

The kids don't get the hang glider sails, but they find a boat. Maybe they will get off the island.

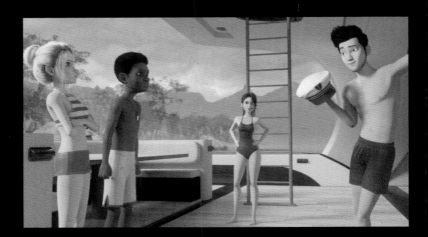

Kenji thinks that all he needs to be captain is a captain's hat.

They get the ship to the island's marina, only to be attacked by dinosaurs.

Brooklynn and Darius try to fix a hole in the boat while the others keep the dinosaurs distracted.

The kids get the boat fixed and running, but the dinosaurs continue their pursuit.

Fireworks frighten the dinosaurs away, and the boat makes its way out to the open ocean.

Finally, Darius and his friends escape the island. But where will their adventures take them now?

slumped to the ground. She took out the antidote and the syringes, and Brooklynn scooped them up.

Brooklynn uncapped a syringe and stuck the needle into the vial of antidote. Then she quickly gave it to Sammy.

Yasmina struggled to get to her feet. Her legs were like rubber. "Come on, come on, come on," she muttered. Somehow, she found the strength to stand and made her way to Sammy. "Please wake up," she whispered. "You have to. You're the best friend I've ever had. Forget what I said. We'll always be friends, no matter how far apart we are. It might not be easy or perfect, but it's worth fighting for. *You're* worth fighting for. You taught me that."

The camp was silent.

Then Sammy suddenly lurched forward, coughing, shivering, as the kids rushed to hug her.

Sammy's eyes opened, and she smiled when she saw Yasmina.

CHAPTER TWELVE

"**H**ow ya feelin'?"

Sitting next to Sammy, Brooklynn held the empty antidote vial in her hand.

"Like I got punched in the stomach by a porcupine," Sammy groaned. "So, ya know, better."

Darius put a hand on Sammy's shoulder, then looked around the camp. Thanks to all the commotion caused by the hybrid, the supplies they had gathered for their trip were scattered everywhere.

"Let's get the food, water, and us to the boat while there's a break in the storm," Darius said.

"What about the Scorpios rex?" Brooklynn asked.

"We have to risk it. We might not get another chance," Darius said grimly.

The kids nodded, and Ben slowly looked toward the foreboding jungle beyond.

"Bumpy," he said softly.

As Sammy recuperated, the others went to work, gathering the necessary supplies for the journey ahead. Water, canned food, walkie-talkies, and spears were rapidly acquired.

Yasmina helped Sammy to her feet. They hugged, and then Sammy slowly started sinking.

"Sorry," Sammy said. "Having a little trouble staying upright."

Yasmina picked Sammy up, putting her arm under Sammy's to keep her upright. "No apology necessary. Whatever you need, I'm here for you. I'm gonna be the *best* best friend ever."

"Where's Ben?" Brooklynn asked.

"Seriously? Again?" Kenji said, annoyed. "We need to put a leash on that kid."

"He knows how dangerous it is!" Darius said. "Why would he just run off like that?"

As Darius started to search the camp, Brooklynn had an aha moment. "Bumpy ran off 'cause of the Scorpios rex. Ben's probably going after her!"

Looking at the ground, Darius saw the stone that Ben used to sharpen his spear. It was close to the edge of the jungle. He picked up the stone and said, "I'm going after him."

The kids raised their voices in protest, but they knew that someone had to find Ben or they couldn't leave.

"Fine," Brooklynn said. "Let's go. The sooner we get Ben, the sooner we get out of here."

"We can't risk all of us," Darius said, shaking his head. "The Scorpios is still out there. I'm going alone."

Brooklynn gave Darius an exasperated look. "Again? You don't always have to do everything alone!"

"Get to the boat," Darius said, determined. "If Ben and I aren't there by sunrise . . . well, you know what that means. And you leave without us."

Again, shouts of protest erupted in the camp. But Darius didn't say anything. He jerked his head quickly, then shushed everyone as he stared into the jungle, pointing.

The group looked at the jungle, certain that the Scorpios rex was going to leap out at any second.

"I don't see anything," Kenji said. He turned around and saw that Darius was gone.

Realizing that Darius had played a trick on them in order to search for Ben, the others groaned.

"What do we do now?" Sammy asked.

Picking up the water jug, Kenji said, "We go to the boat."

Darius made sure the walkie-talkie was in his pocket. He was on high alert, scanning the ground for footprints, plants that looked like they had been stepped on—anything that might point the way to Ben. And the Scorpios rex was never far from his thoughts.

After a moment, Darius stopped. The trail seemed to disappear in a leafy patch.

"Ben!" Darius called out. There was silence for a moment, and then came the sound of something very large stomping through the jungle.

"Stupid Darius thinking we're going to stupid leave without him on that stupid boat," Kenji said.

"Don't worry," Brooklynn said. "Kid's got major FOMO. He'll make it there by sunrise."

Kenji suddenly pointed in front of them. "But will *we*?"

Brooklynn saw what Kenji was pointing at. There were smashed flowers and crushed plants everywhere. All the landmarks they had used before to help find their way to the yacht were now gone. It seemed clear that the herd of dinosaurs, the ones that had been so spooked by the Scorpios rex, had come this way, trampling everything in their path.

"Stupid Scorpios rex messing up the stupid path to the stupid boat," Kenji said.

The kids looked at one another, realizing they had no idea where they were. Sammy began to whimper.

"Don't worry," Yasmina said, seeing that Sammy was starting to give in to her worst fears. Taking a deep breath, she added brightly, "We believe in you guys! You'll figure it out!"

Kenji wrinkled his brow and whispered to Brooklynn, "Did she just . . . encourage us?"

"I can't tell," Brooklynn whispered back.

"Any of this look familiar to you?" Kenji asked.

The kids had been wandering for a while now, trying to see if anything would jog their memory and tell them which way they should go.

Brooklynn dropped her tote bags, frustrated. "Nope," she said.

Kenji closed his eyes, thinking. "Whenever we're on our way to the boat, Darius is always like, 'Did you know Stegosauruses pull bark off the trees to blah, blah, blah' . . . because he always sees that tree with the missing bark!"

His eyes popped open, and Kenji looked excited. "Which should be just through . . ."

Then he rushed ahead, poking through some shrubs, into a small clearing.

"Here!"

There was the tree with the missing bark, sure enough! Except the tree was now laying on its side, blocking their path. All around it, there were more downed trees, broken branches, and long, gnarled roots. With rocks and jungle on either side, it seemed quite impassable.

"Great," Sammy said. "How are we gonna get past this?"

"Don't sweat it!" Yasmina said. "Kenji's on to something! He's doing a great job. He'll figure out a way, won't ya, Kenji?"

"I dunno," Kenji said, a little freaked out. "Maybe? Finding it hard to concentrate with Yaz supporting me."

"Right?" Brooklynn said in agreement. "Let's just try to clear a path."

There was another loud roar, and Darius nestled in against some tree roots. Was it the Scorpios rex?

He raised his head just a little and poked it out

to see a lone Sinoceratops emerge, whipping its tail, moving in circles. Relieved, he began to climb out and noticed that there was a quill sticking out of its tail—the quill of the Scorpios rex.

The dinosaur started to slow down, huffing. Darius moved closer to the creature, and he slowly reached out and pulled the quill free! Tossing it aside, Darius was stunned to see the Sinoceratops spin around and charge at him!

Darius scrambled through the tree roots as the Sinoceratops gave chase. It went around the tree, while Darius went under, emerging on the other side into thick foliage.

He was way ahead of the Sinoceratops. Then he pivoted and saw that he was right on the edge of the drop-off! He nearly slid over the side but caught himself at the last second.

He heard a grunting sound and turned to see the Sinoceratops no longer charging at him. The dinosaur was weaving back and forth as if it was finally feeling the full effects of the Scorpios rex's poison. Darius walked over, putting his hands on the creature, trying to soothe it.

"Easy," Darius said. "Easy."

The Sinoceratops no longer seemed aggressive. Then it wandered away, and Darius finally was able to relax. Which is exactly when the soft ground beneath his feet gave way, and he plunged straight off the cliff. Darius screamed and threw a hand up, hoping to find something to grab on to. But something reached out and grabbed *him.*

It was Ben! He had Darius by the arm and hauled him up over the side of the cliff. They collapsed on the ground.

"So we'll meet the others at the boat," Darius said as he struggled to keep up with Ben. "If we go now, we'll be there way before sunrise."

Ben stopped for a second, looked around, and then pushed ahead. Darius was confused.

"Uh, Ben . . . boat's back this way," Darius said.

But Ben didn't reply. He just kept on walking.

"Hello? Ben? Are you even listening?"

Ben stopped again, and Darius caught up to him, panting. He could tell that Ben still wasn't paying attention to him.

"Ben, stop! Look, I know . . . Bumpy could be anywhere."

"Exactly," Ben said, finally acknowledging Darius. "She could be wherever the Scorpios rex is. I need to find her before it does. You wanna go to the boat, go. No one's stopping you."

Then Ben took off into the jungle.

Darius knew he didn't have a choice.

He followed Ben.

"You're doing a bang-up job!" Yasmina said as Kenji tried to get away from her. "We just gotta keep our chins up!"

So far, the group had managed to clear exactly none of the debris blocking their way.

Brooklynn approached Yasmina and pulled her aside. "Yaz, I know you're just trying to help or . . . whatever it is you're doing, but can you stop? It's freaking us out!"

Yasmina whispered in Brooklynn's ear. "Sammy needs me to stay positive!" Then she turned to look at her friends and gave them a big forced smile.

"Trust me, she does not need *that*," Brooklynn said. "None of us do! We just need you to be *you*!"

Yasmina was about to say something when Sammy pointed off into the darkness. "Am I about to lose consciousness, or do y'all see those glowing fairies, too?"

Kenji turned and saw what looked like dancing lights in the distance. "I'm deffo seeing it, too."

The blurs of light appeared to be growing larger as Brooklynn said, "Wait a minute . . . aren't those—"

"The Parasaurolophuses!" Yasmina jumped in. "From the caves!"

A small herd of bioluminescent Parasaurolophuses came into view and joined them in the clearing.

"Why'd they leave their home to come all the way out here?" Sammy asked.

Suddenly, the Parasaurolophuses began to wail and stomp their feet.

The kids didn't need another sign. They dove behind some large rocks, slowly peering around the side . . . only to hear the awful shriek of the Scorpios rex.

"Shhhh," Ben said, pointing at a drool-covered bush as it shook.

"Scorpios?" Darius asked.

"No," Ben said. "Its steps aren't that heavy. I think it's—"

Ben spun around just as Bumpy bolted from a stand of nearby trees.

"Bumpy!" he shouted. "You're safe!"

"Glad you're okay, girl," Darius said as he patted Bumpy on her head. "We were worried. Now let's all get to the boat before—"

"I . . . I'm not going with you," Ben said.

Darius put up his hands like he was giving up. "Fine, stay mad at me. We don't have to walk together. I'll stay ten paces behind you. Cool? It doesn't matter how we get to the boat, just that we get there."

Ben moved closer and looked Darius right in the eye. "No . . . I'm not leaving the island."

"Bumpy fits on the boat, and Bumpy is with us now," Darius said, frustrated. "Ergo, boat time for all of us."

"It was never just about Bumpy," Ben replied. "It's about me, too. I need to stay. This is my home. I'm happy here! I've got grubs. I've got Bumpy. I've got the thick jungle air. I'm more me on this island than I've ever been. The best version of me!"

Shaking his head, Darius said, "You'll never make it!"

"You know that's not true," Ben said. "Why don't you trust me?"

"Because you're just a kid! You don't know *anything* about surviving out here!"

"Yes, I do! I did it before, and I can certainly do it again."

The words hit Darius hard. The only reason Ben had to survive in the jungle in the first place was because he fell from the monorail.

"Enough!" Darius shouted. "This is ridiculous. I tried being patient, but we're out of time."

Bumpy brayed as Ben said, "Darius, you're not listening—"

"No, *you're* not listening!" Darius fired back.

"I'm sorry you're not happy with my decision, but it's not up to you!" Ben said.

Ben took off, brushing past Darius, bumping his shoulder. He stopped, then turned to look at his friend, offering his hand. "Now, let's just—"

But he wasn't able to finish his sentence, because Darius had already tackled him to the ground. Darius pinned him down, but Ben was able to wriggle free. Now Ben took Darius down. The walkie-talkie that had been in Darius's pocket fell out, hitting the ground with a loud CRACK.

"I'm trying to help you!" Darius shouted.

"By controlling me?"

Ben tried to get away, but Darius grabbed his ankle, pulling him back. Then they both got to their feet.

"I'm not abandoning you!" Darius yelled.

Ben was about to say something, but he just couldn't find the words. The two boys stared at each other, not talking, not fighting . . . just staring.

The silence was broken by Bumpy. She bleated again.

Ben walked over to her and said, "Sorry you had to see that, Bumpers. Darius and I are just . . . working through some stuff."

Darius took a breath, then picked up the walkie-talkie from the ground. He heard another bleating sound and looked up. It wasn't Bumpy.

He and Ben turned around to see that Bumpy was no longer alone. Standing next to Darius was an Ankylosaurus that was nuzzling Bumpy. Then another Ankylosaurus appeared, and another. In no time, a small group of dinosaurs had gathered around Bumpy.

"Looks like Bumpy found her herd," Darius said.

CHAPTER THIRTEEN

The Parasaurolophuses were stomping around, frightened, as Kenji, Brooklynn, Yasmina, and Sammy did their best to stay hidden by the rocks.

The roar of the Scorpius rex thundered throughout the jungle. It spooked one of the Parasaurolophuses so much that the dinosaur charged the trees blocking the way. A shower of splintered wood and logs followed as the kids ducked.

Yasmina looked at her friends and saw Kenji, afraid. Sammy was holding her stomach, looking weak, worried.

She knew what she had to do . . . and how she had to do it.

"Kenji! Do your job and get us outta here!" she yelled.

Kenji snapped to attention. That was the old Yasmina, the one he knew. He immediately perked up and looked at the Parasaurolophuses as they smashed into the trees.

"They're making a path!" he said. "Follow the glowy dinos!"

Kenji jumped behind a Parasaurolophus. Kenji was carrying the jug of water.

Sammy got to her feet and gave Yasmina a worried look. "I don't know if I can do this."

Yasmina crossed her arms and stared at Sammy. "I ran from the Indominus rex on a busted-up ankle, so you're not getting off the hook that easy, slacker. Come on!"

"Right," Sammy said, setting her jaw. "Let's go!"

Sammy leaped right behind another Parasaurolophus. Brooklynn grinned at Yasmina, holding her hand out for a fist bump. But Yasmina pushed her forward instead. "Go!"

"Right, duh," Brooklynn said, picking up the remaining supplies with Yasmina.

They made it to the other side of the trees, where they saw Kenji waiting for them. He pointed off in the distance. Sammy was already ahead of them.

"I know where we are!" Kenji said. "The dock is that way!"

In no time, Yasmina and Brooklynn caught up with Sammy. Kenji was not far behind. A Parasaurolophus was keeping pace with them.

Kenji squinted his eyes, looking ahead. "Should just be right—"

Suddenly, the dinosaur squealed!

Startled, the kids saw the Scorpios rex with the limp Parasaurolophus in its deadly grip.

Putting a finger to her lips, Brooklynn motioned everyone toward the dense foliage near them. The dinosaur didn't seem to notice them at all as the walking horror dragged its prey into the jungle.

Taking the chance while they had it, the kids sprinted toward the dock.

"Darius!" The voice came over his walkie-talkie while Darius sat next to Ben on a log, watching Bumpy playing with the larger Ankylosauruses.

"Brooklynn!" Darius replied, talking into the receiver. "Brooklynn!"

But the button was jammed. He couldn't send!

"Darius, do you copy?" Brooklynn asked over the crackling radio.

"Musta broken during the fight," Darius said.

"And whose fault was that?" Ben teased.

"Darius, if you can hear me, we just had a run-in with the Scorpios, but everyone's okay. We're headed to the boat now, should be there any minute."

Darius looked at the walkie-talkie, then turned to face Ben.

"He probably just turned it off so we don't bug him," Kenji said to Brooklynn. "Darius and Ben . . . they'll be okay."

Kenji then pushed away the tree branches in front of them. They could see the dock, with the yacht moving up and down as the waves lapped up against the shore.

"And I thought finding this boat the first time was the happiest I'd ever be to see it. Would it be weird if I hugged it? That'd be weird, right? I'm gonna hug it," Sammy said.

Sammy walked right over to the boat and, as promised, hugged it.

"Sammy's back, folks!" Brooklynn said.

Yasmina looked at her best friend and smiled. Then she turned to Kenji. "I'd tell you how proud I am of you, but I don't want to freak you out."

"Please don't ever do that again," Kenji replied. "We need your patented snark to keep us motivated."

"Noted," Yasmina said.

Darius looked up at the sky and could tell that dawn was approaching. Then he looked over at Ben. Neither one of them had said anything about the future following their fight. Darius wasn't sure what was supposed to happen now.

He noticed that the herd of Ankylosauruses began to move about, agitated. They started bleating. Darius shot Ben a look, but before they could do anything, the Scorpios rex appeared, jumping over a log, zooming right over their heads, and moving straight for the clearing . . . and the Ankylosaurus herd.

"Bumpy! Watch out!" Ben cried.

He pushed forward, but Darius caught him. "You can't help her!" Darius said.

The Ankylosauruses were now circling, forming a tight pack around Bumpy.

"But they might be able to!" Darius added.

The Ankylosauruses suddenly dropped to the ground, with their thick, bony backs forming a shield.

The Scorpios rex snarled at the dinosaurs, swiping at the Ankylosauruses. But it was unable to reach Bumpy. Then it jumped into the air and, landing in the middle of the formation, attacked Bumpy! The Ankylosauruses saw this and started swiping their tails against the twisted creature. The Scorpios rex staggered and fell to the ground.

It struggled to its feet, taking more swipes at the Ankylosauruses. It attacked with its quills, hitting one larger dinosaur. Another got quilled in the leg.

But the Ankylosauruses weren't giving up. As soon as one was struck down, another strong, healthy one took its place. They continued to batter the Scorpios rex with their tails. One of the Ankylosauruses got the hybrid right in the face, and the Scorpios rex flew back, landing on a rock, shrieking in pain.

It got up from the rock slowly, snarling, and then it retreated into the trees.

Ben and Darius waited, but the Scorpios rex didn't return.

"They did it!" Ben shouted.

"Wait . . . if Brooklynn and the others just ran into the Scorpios rex . . . and it's all the way over here now . . . it's gotta be the fastest dinosaur ever," Darius said.

Ben nodded and watched as the herd of Ankylosauruses circled around, licking their wounds and checking on one another.

"You were right, Darius," Ben said. "The herd can protect Bumpy in a way I can't. She belongs with them." Tears formed in his eyes as he said, "I have to let her go."

He wiped away the tears and faced Darius.

"Saying goodbye is never easy," Darius said. "But

you're being a good friend. You're doing what's best for her."

"So why can't you do that for me?" Ben said. "Staying here *is* what's best for me."

Darius shook his head. "No! I let you go once on the monorail, and then . . . everything you had to go through, running from who knows how many dinosaurs, all those cold nights with no food . . . was because of me. It's why I can't leave you here."

Ben put a hand on Darius's shoulder and said, "None of that was your fault. All you've ever done is try to protect me, all of us. I'm not mad at you. I never was. I . . . I love you, bud."

Surprised, Darius found himself wiping a tear from his eyes. "We're quite a pair, huh?"

The two hugged, and Darius said, "Come to the boat with me and tell everyone goodbye. You owe them that."

"Deal," Ben said.

At last, Darius let go, and they headed for the yacht.

The sun had just started to come up as Kenji, Brooklynn, Yasmina, and Sammy stood on the deck of the yacht.

"We're not leaving without them," Kenji said. "No matter what."

The group stared at the jungle, anxiously awaiting the arrival of their missing friends. At last, the foliage began to shake.

"Look!" Kenji shouted. "Darius! Ben! Told you we'd never leave you guys!"

The rustling grew closer and closer.

Darius and Ben burst through the foliage, and both were breathing hard from running. Darius grinned as he looked down at the dock and saw that the yacht was—gone.

"Wow," Darius said, stunned. "I . . . I really thought they'd wait."

A terrifying roar came from behind, and Darius and Ben froze in their tracks. Slowly, they turned around and saw the Scorpios rex come out of the jungle on their left.

Then came another roar.

And a second Scorpios rex, smaller than the first one, appeared on their right.

Darius and Ben were now trapped between the two terrifying hybrids.

"There's two of them?!" they said in unison as the Scorpios rexes roared.

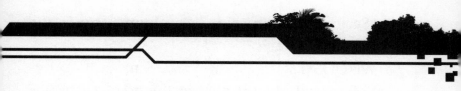

CHAPTER FOURTEEN

Darius and Ben were caught right in the middle of the Scorpios rexes, quite certain that this was the end. There would be no escaping the raging dinosaurs.

The creatures snarled and charged right at the boys.

It took Darius and Ben a second to realize that the dinosaurs weren't charging them. They were running toward each other!

"C'mon!" Darius shouted as he and Ben sprinted away. Looking over his shoulder, Darius saw the two Scorpios rexes fighting—claws flashing, jaws snapping, feet stomping.

"Over here!" Ben hollered as he pulled Darius toward the limousine, the same one they had taken from Kenji's penthouse down to the dock.

Ben tried to open the door, but it was locked.

"Seriously?" Ben said. "Who locks a car in the middle of the jungle?!"

WHOOSH!

Before Darius could answer, the tail of a Scorpios rex whipped right above them. The boys managed to duck just in time. Then Darius tackled Ben to the ground, but this time there was no fight. He pulled Ben underneath the limousine for cover as the two dinosaurs continued their war.

A moment later, the car was shredded in half and tossed into the jungle clearing. The boys were now laying on the ground, staring up at the Scorpios rexes as they fought one another.

"Look!" Darius shouted. He pointed to the limousine.

One of the windows had been smashed open in the chaos. Darius and Ben sprinted away from the dueling dinosaurs and dove into the limousine through the broken window. Again, the Scorpios rex swiped with its tail, and again, they narrowly missed getting clocked by it.

"What are you doing?" Ben said as Darius buckled his seat belt.

"Reflex," Darius said, embarrassed.

One of the Scorpius rexes roared loudly, and the whole limousine seemed to shake. Nervous, Ben buckled his seat belt, too.

Suddenly, the fighting dinosaurs jumped on top of the limousine, causing the car to spin around and shake nearly to pieces. The boys screamed, hanging on as the limousine went topsy-turvy. Then there was a loud CRUNCH, the sound of metal being crumpled. A Scorpios rex bellowed.

And then it was quiet.

The dinosaurs weren't fighting.

Darius and Ben took a deep breath and realized for the first time that the limousine was now completely vertical, with the hood smashed into the ground. They were dangling from their seat belts, still safe.

"Kenji forgot his hat," Ben said, noticing it on the rearview mirror.

Darius smiled and took the captain's hat.

"At least the others got away," Darius said with a sigh.

"Aw, man, I left my captain's hat in the limo!" Kenji said as he stood behind the wheel of the yacht, cursing his luck. "But at least, I locked the door. It'll be safe."

"Uh, Kenji?" Yasmina said. "I think we have slightly bigger problems."

The yacht was now on the open sea, away from Kenji's penthouse, the dock, the shore, and Isla Nublar.

"Yeah, there's that thing where we left our friends on a dinosaur-infested island?" Brooklynn reminded Kenji.

"I know, I know. We're heading back to the dock." Kenji said.

"What if the only thing waiting there for them is the Scorpios rex?" Brooklynn asked, worried.

Kenji knew that Brooklynn was right. They had to go back and get their friends.

Ben was sitting next to the smashed limousine. Darius paced back and forth, holding Kenji's captain's hat.

"How are there *two* of that thing?!" Ben said in disbelief.

"Yeah," Darius said. "My theory is that since all the dinosaurs have other animals' DNA built into their genetic code, like tree frogs, some of which can reproduce asexually—"

"The only thing more terrifying than one psycho dinosaur is two that can make more of themselves whenever they want!" Ben said with a shudder.

"We gotta do something fast," Darius said.

"They don't seem to get along too well," Ben observed. "Maybe they'll just take each other out?"

"We can't count on that," Darius said. He paused for a moment and then looked at Ben. "I'm gonna stop them. Once and for all."

Ben nodded. "So, how we gonna do it? With explosions?" he said eagerly.

Shaking his head, Darius said, "First, we need to disable them somehow, knock them out maybe. And to do that, we gotta go back to where it all began."

He looked out at the jungle and put the captain's hat on his head. Then Darius started off into the jungle.

"And? Is there a part B to that idea?" Ben asked. "Like maybe . . . 'blow something up'?"

Darius didn't reply. He only walked forward, and Ben ran to catch up with him.

They had only been in the jungle for about a minute when the yacht appeared on the horizon, approaching the dock.

"Oh my gosh! Guys!"

The yacht had pulled into the pier, and the kids had disembarked. Sammy had run ahead toward the jungle and was motioning toward the others.

"What is it?" Kenji asked. "Describe it with words."

"Just walk over here, Kenji!" she yelled.

Kenji groaned and then followed Brooklynn and Yasmina into the jungle, where they found Sammy standing near the limousine that was sticking up in the ground. There were footprints all over the vehicle.

The footprints of the Scorpios rex.

"Oh no," Brooklynn said. "Did Darius and Ben . . . ?"

"They got away!" Sammy said, pointing at two sets of human footprints on the ground leading away from the much larger Scorpios rex footprints, into the jungle.

"That's gotta be them!" Brooklynn said.

"Okay," Kenji said. "New plan. We find Darius and Ben before we all get eaten by dinosaurs. In and out. No messin' around."

The kids took off running.

In the distance, the roars of the two Scorpios rexes could be heard, their battle clearly still raging.

Darius and Ben were in the thick of the jungle now, moving as fast as they could. There was a faint sound up ahead, and Darius stopped to listen. Ben did the same.

It was a crashing sound, and it seemed to be getting closer. Then there was a noise, almost like a trumpet, or a—

"Brachiosaurus," Ben said.

The crashing was getting louder now, and closer, and there were even more trumpeting sounds.

CRASH!

A large tree fell, and the trees around the boys were all shaking. More trees fell, and it became instantly clear that nowhere was safe.

Darius and Ben looked at each other with panic in their eyes. Should they run? Where to? They looked around, but there was no obvious shelter and nowhere to run to.

The crashing grew even louder, and the ground was shaking as a herd of Brachiosauruses broke through the trees, moving fast, making their trumpeting sounds as if they were an alarm.

Trees splintered, falling into other trees, and like dominoes, they started to topple.

The boys ducked, rolled, covered, and somehow managed to get out of the way of the thundering herd.

At last, they stood up and watched the herd stampede into the jungle, leaving a trail of destruction.

"Where's the ol' Scorpios rexies?" Ben said.

"Let's not stick around to find out," Darius said, and they trudged back into the jungle.

"More footprints—over here!" Sammy called out.

She was standing in a jungle clearing, with downed trees everywhere, and trampled brush.

"Whooooa," Yasmina said. "Something big came through here. Like, *lots* of something bigs."

Brooklynn looked closely at the ground, observing the footprints.

"Brachiosaurus stampede?" she suggested.

"So?" Kenji said. "We're looking for Ben and Darius, remember? That's just dinosaurs doing dinosaur stuff."

"No, they destroyed the trees they like to eat," Sammy countered. "Something spooked 'em real bad!"

"Had to be the Scorpios rex," Brooklynn said. "It's gonna kill every other dinosaur on this island. On purpose or by starving them or scaring them into places they shouldn't be!"

"So what?" Kenji protested. "Why should we care what happens to the dinosaurs?"

"Because." Brooklynn shrugged. She paused as she struggled to collect her thoughts and find the right words. "Because *life,* Kenji. It's worth protecting. The Scorpios was never meant to be out in the wild. Dr. Wu knew that when he froze it. It's not a dinosaur. It's a monster."

Sammy, Yasmina, and Brooklynn turned around to stare at Kenji.

"Okay, yeah, obviously this Scorpios thing is bad," Kenji said. "But it's not our responsibility. Wu and the people who made that freak shoulda thought of the consequences before they gene-spliced a buncha random lizards together!"

"Yeah, but—" Brooklynn started.

"But nothing! We need to focus on finding Darius and Ben. In and out. And then—finally—we escape this nightmare island!"

Brooklynn opened her mouth to speak but noticed a high-pitched whining sound. Everyone froze and looked around.

"I swear, if that's the Scorpios rex . . . ," Kenji said.

Following the sound of the whining, the kids walked to the other side of a fallen log . . . where they found a baby Brachiosaurus.

There was a collective "Awww!" as Sammy carefully approached the baby with outstretched hands.

"Sammy, don't touch—"

Too late. Sammy was already petting the Brachiosaurus.

"Okay, nobody else—"

And now Brooklynn and Yasmina were petting the baby, too.

"Guys, in and out, remember?" Kenji said, trying

to keep the plan on track.

"She's looking for her herd," Sammy said.

"That's very nice for her, but—"

The baby whined, and Kenji's eyes went wide.

"I can't believe I'm—"

Then Kenji put his hands to his mouth and imitated the loud, trumpet-like call of the Brachiosaurus.

The girls were amazed and stared at Kenji.

"What?" he said. "I got layers."

The girls smiled at him and put their hands to their mouths, too, making trumpet-like sounds.

A moment later, two Brachiosaurus heads popped up above the treetops, just beyond the clearing. They trumpeted in response!

Trees swayed as a huge Brachiosaurus emerged from the jungle. It bent its long neck to the ground and touched noses with the infant dinosaur.

Kenji was now crying and sniffling as Brooklynn gave him a glance.

"Allergies," Kenji said.

No one believed it.

They watched as the adult Brachiosaurus led the baby back into the jungle. But something else caught Yasmina's attention. She looked at the ground and picked it up.

"Whoa," Kenji said, looking at what Yasmina had found. "That looks exactly like my captain's hat!"

"It is your captain's hat!" Yasmina said. "Darius and Ben must have brought it here. Which means we're still heading the right way!"

"Up here!" Yasmina shouted, smiling. "More footprints!"

The other kids grinned as they ran after Yasmina.

But by the time Sammy, Brooklynn, and Kenji had caught up to her, Yasmina's smile was gone.

"Yaz, what is it?" Sammy asked.

Yasmina pointed at the ground. The human footprints they had been following now merged with two sets of dinosaur footprints.

Scorpios rex footprints.

"The guys must be tracking the Scorpios," Yasmina said.

"Or . . . the Scorpios is tracking them," Sammy said.

Darius checked the area as he and Ben walked past the Jurassic Park Visitor Center and into the overgrown jungle nearby. They came upon the overturned 4x4.

"Looking for berries?" Ben said, watching Darius. "Better lemme handle it. I know the difference between the poisonous red ones and the not-poisonous red ones."

But Darius wasn't paying attention to Ben. He pointed. "There!"

It was the tranquilizer rifle!

"Right where we left it," Darius said. "Let's hope it works."

Darius went to pick up the tranquilizer, but before he could reach it, he heard a rustling sound coming from some bushes.

The boys turned around, expecting dinosaurs.

Instead, it was Brooklynn, Sammy, Yasmina, and Kenji!

"Thank goodness we found you!" Sammy said.

"What are you guys doing here?" he said, incredulous. "We thought you left!"

"What?" Kenji said in disbelief. "No! Camp fam for life, right? We'd never leave someone behind!"

Everyone nodded, and Darius glanced at Ben as if to say, "See?"

"We just had to get away from that stupid Scorpios," Kenji continued. "It was on the dock."

"Yeah, we saw them up close and personal," Darius said.

"Hold up," Sammy interjected. " 'Them'?"

"There's two of them," Ben confirmed.

"Yeah, and unless we take them out, they're gonna destroy everything and everyone," Darius said.

All eyes were on Kenji now. "I don't want to be

on this island a second longer than I have to be," he said. "But it's like I always say. Life is worth protecting."

Brooklynn smiled and elbowed Kenji.

"Okay, then," Darius said, picking up the tranquilizer rifle. "Let's go find a Scorpios rex."

A splash of rain hit Darius. Ben saw it and felt an icy chill run up his spine.

It wasn't rain. It was drool.

A Scorpios rex was sitting in the tree right above them.

The kids entered the Visitor Center, the hybrid right behind them. They locked the door just as the Scorpios rex arrived. The creature rammed the door, and the walls shook as it roared in anger.

Then they heard a purring sound. They saw something creeping in through a crack in the wall.

The second Scorpios rex.

WHAM!

The first hybrid slammed against the door.

The second one growled, coming closer.

"It's the only way," Darius said, grasping the tranquilizer rifle. He closed his eyes and squeezed the trigger.

And totally missed.

The second Scorpios rex charged right for them, and the group scattered.

As Darius attempted to load another tranquilizer dart, the second hybrid swiped at him with its fearsome tail. Darius fell, dropping the dart and the rifle. Before he could reach them, the second hybrid crashed into the scaffolding. The scaffold shattered, pieces going everywhere.

"This way!" Kenji said, pointing to a hallway.

The second Scorpios rex, temporarily blinded, smashed into more scaffolding. The kids regrouped and ran for the hallway.

"Shhhhh," Brooklynn said as they entered what look like a big stainless-steel kitchen, full of rusty, dented cabinets.

Kenji went behind the counter, waving the others to his side. They crouched down next to a bunch of rusty kitchen utensils.

"What now?" Brooklynn whispered.

A rustling sound came from the hallway. They heard the clatter of the Scorpios rex's claws on the tile floor outside.

Then they saw its shadow through the window, its breath fogging the glass.

They stared at the door and watched the handle, praying it wouldn't turn.

It didn't.

They heard the clicking sound again. It was walking away!

Darius closed his eyes and sighed.

Which is exactly when the second Scorpios rex crashed through the wall.

The beast tore through the kitchen, shrieking, snapping its jaws. The kids raced through the broken door and back into the main room. Compys were everywhere, trying to get away from the mayhem.

"Outside!" Kenji called, and he threw open the front door, holding it. The others ran through. Kenji closed the door and ran.

But there was another dinosaur blocking their path.

A blue Velociraptor.

The dinosaur snarled at the kids and took a step forward. The group backed up through the front door and right back into the Visitor Center.

The blue Velociraptor pushed the doors open and crept inside. The second Scorpios rex took notice and snarled at the new arrival.

The Compys fled as the hybrid lost interest in them. The creature was now squaring off against the Velociraptor, with the kids stuck right in the middle.

"We're trapped," Brooklynn said.

Thinking fast, Yasmina pointed to the roof.

She made a move for the scaffolding to start climbing, but a sharp roar from above made it clear that something else was already there.

A Scorpios rex was on the roof! It was shrieking, snapping its jaws, and shoving its head into the main room. Debris fell from the weight of the dinosaur on the roof.

Darius gulped and took a step backward—but something was beneath his foot. He looked down and saw the tranquilizer rifle! He went to pick it up but froze when he realized that the Velociraptor was watching him.

Locking eyes with the dinosaur, Darius slowly pulled his hand away from the tranquilizer rifle and stood up. Then he raised his hands in surrender.

Both Scorpios rexes roared.

And then the Velociraptor blinked at Darius as it sprung forward! The creature jumped right over them and landed on the second Scorpios rex!

As the Velociraptor and the second hybrid fought, they knocked into the walls and the scaffolding. The entire building shook, and beams above creaked from the stress. Debris fell from the roof as the first Scorpios rex went wild, spoiling to join the fight below.

"We gotta go," Sammy said. "If the roof collapses on us, we're toast."

Darius looked at her and smiled. "But they would be, too."

He ran over to the scaffolding and began to kick at it.

"Help me!" he screamed.

The kids looked at each other, instantly realizing the plan. They ran over to Darius, dodging falling debris, right past the Velociraptor–Scorpios rex fight.

"C'mon!" Darius said, throwing his weight against the scaffolding. "We gotta take this whole place down!"

The kids joined in, pushing their backs into the scaffolding. The structure, already weakened, was creaking loudly, and then it fell right over, smashing into more scaffolding on the way down.

"Run for it, now!" Darius ordered, and everyone bolted for the door.

The building groaned, shuddering—it was about to fall!

Beams fell from the ceiling, jailing the second hybrid.

Darius turned around to see the blue Velociraptor. He wanted to tell her to leave, too. Then she cocked her head and jumped over debris, landing right in front of Darius! His eyes went wide, and the blue Velociraptor snarled at him before running off into the jungle.

He looked up to see the first Scorpios rex on the roof, just as it was caving in. The hybrid fell right on top of the second Scorpios rex, and the two lashed out at each other one last time.

The entire building collapsed on them, and there was one final earsplitting shriek . . . then silence.

The kids stared at the rubble. They all felt a bit of sadness, but Darius seemed the saddest to see the original dream for the Park so utterly in ruin. Ben put a hand on Darius's shoulder and smiled. "Come on, I'll walk you to the boat."

"Welp," Ben said. "This is it, huh?"

He was standing on the dock, looking at his friends.

"I know I've already asked you this like a hundred times on the walk back," Sammy said. "But . . . are you sure you wanna stay behind, Ben?"

Ben nodded.

"You guys are my family, but . . . this island is home. I know how to survive here. I—I found myself here."

Sammy took Ben's hand and gave it a squeeze. "But every time I think of you out here all alone, my heart hurts."

"And I'll miss you," Yasmina said.

"We'll *all* miss you," Brooklynn affirmed.

Kenji walked over to Ben. "I get that you have to do this for you, but did you ever think about what it would do to us? We'll never stop worrying about you, you jerk."

"You don't have to worry about me," Ben said.

Now Darius put a hand on his shoulder. "But we will. Because we're a family. Being apart won't change that."

Ben felt his throat tighten, and he looked at Darius. A light rain began to fall—definitely rain, not dinosaur drool—and Ben wondered if he was making the right decision.

"Wind's picking up," he said. "Another storm is on the way. Best sail out before it rolls in."

The others started to protest, not wanting to leave Ben. But Darius interrupted. "Come on, guys. Ben's made up his made. We gotta respect it."

As the kids boarded the yacht, Ben watched them. He saw Kenji put on his captain's hat and start the engine.

Everyone waved goodbye, tears in their eyes.

"Stay safe, Ben!" Darius called out.

"We love you!" Sammy said.

Ben waved back, uncertain. "Love ya, too," he muttered.

"Are we really doing this?" Sammy asked. "Are we really leaving him here?"

The yacht pulled away from the dock, but Darius didn't answer Sammy's question. He just stared at Ben, watching his friend grow smaller and smaller.

"Come on," Darius said.

It grew quiet, and then Darius heard it. Someone . . . yelling?

"Guys!"

Darius stared more intently at the dock. He saw Ben sprinting down the dock.

"Guys! Wait!"

Everyone on board realized exactly what was happening, and their smiles were contagious.

"Kenji! Kill the engine!" Darius said.

Then Ben dove into the ocean and started swimming for the yacht!

A minute later, Darius threw his hand over the side of the yacht and pulled Ben aboard.

Dripping wet, Ben grinned. "I guess I realized that since I 'found myself' on the island, I can take that newfound self somewhere else now."

The group all smiled knowingly at Ben, except for Sammy.

"You guys don't look surprised to see me," he said, puzzled.

"Darius said you'd change your mind," Brooklynn replied.

"Yeah, man," Kenji added. "Didn't think you'd actually go diving in the ocean, though."

Ben looked at Darius, shaking his head. "I—"

"Needed to come to it on your own, without someone telling you how to feel. I know," Darius said, clapping Ben on the back. "Took you long enough!"

Sammy looked bewildered. "Seriously, no one could have clued me in? Oh well." Then she threw her arms around Ben in a big bear hug as the others jumped in for the same.

"Camp Cretaceous, united again!" Sammy shouted.

They heard the rumble of thunder in the distance. Kenji broke from the huddle and climbed the ladder to the bridge to take the wheel.

"Okay, once and for all, let's get outta this dang place!" Kenji said.

"Costa Rica, here we come!" Brooklynn said.

"If we're lucky, we'll be there by morning!" Darius said, practically laughing.

The yacht was moving out to sea when, suddenly,

a blinding spotlight enveloped their vessel.

The kids looked up, surprised to hear the whirring of . . . was it . . . a helicopter? It was! And it wasn't alone. Two more helicopters flew past, moving toward Isla Nublar.

There were two people inside the helicopter that hovered directly above them. They looked to be wearing body armor of some kind, and they had weapons.

"Attention," came a voice over a loudspeaker. "You on the boat. Return to the dock and cut the engine. Immediately."

"Who are these guys?" Darius asked.

The End?

JURASSIC WORLD
CAMP CRETACEOUS
Books that have BITE!

HIDDEN HUNTERS!

LOST IN THE WILD!

WELCOME TO CAMP!

rhcbooks.com